THE CARVER DEVICE

The Carver Device

STEVE MACFARLANE

About the author

Steve Macfarlane is a writer, musician and resident of Tasmania, the land under the land down under. He is usually writing, creating music, thinking about things too deeply and pursuing research into his lifelong quest for understanding. After many years, he transitioned from a moustache to a beard, a testament to his ever-evolving style.

Copyright information

ISBN 978-1-7637099-2-8 (eBook)
ISBN 978-1-7637099-3-5 (Paperback)

CONTENTS

1   **Wendy's story**   1

2   **Countdown**   5

3   **Carols**   9

4   **The older Carol explains**   11

5   **Carol in the future**   15

6   **The briefing**   17

7   **Mission One**   21

8   **Outside the Solar System**   25

9   **What can we do about it?**   27

10   **Is this for real?**   31

11   **Final minutes before the fleet arrives**   33

12   **The message**   37

13   **Lots of questions**   41

14	An alien view of Earth's history	45
15	A bold plan	49
16	The Day of the explosion	53
17	The response	57
18	Rescue	59
19	Commander Epsom reports	67
20	The first depart	73
21	The truth revealed	77
22	Digesting the information	81
23	Coffee break	83
24	The Second Mission	87
25	The Third Expedition	89
26	Darec explains how the AIs began	97
27	A human in 2073	109
28	Back in the classroom	121
29	The history of the future One-I	123
30	An idea	131
31	It's a matter of trust	137

32 **Summary of Day One** **141**

33 **After class** **149**

Prologue 151
Chapter notes 159
Acknowledgements 173

| 1 |

Wendy's story

2021

My best friend was in a terrible state. The worst I'd seen since the disappearance. After two years there was still no news, ransom demand or bodies found. How do you help when your best friend is so badly broken that you worry they'll give in to a spiralling depression and take their own life to end the pain?

Drinking.

We'd started with a good red wine and then moved on to a second bottle and were eyeing the third. I don't remember what it was. It may have been that expensive stuff. I wasn't really paying attention. It was going down very easily. As we went over the circumstances for the umpteenth time, nothing became any clearer except that our desire to understand what happened two years ago hadn't diminished.

Losing your whole family in an accident like a car crash is terrible but at least you know where they are and what happened. It was the driver's fault or the other driver's fault... or just a complete unlucky accident. Wrong place, wrong time. When they disappear without explanation and the police investigators have no idea what happened, it takes you to a darker place. At least it did to my best friend.

We'd known each other since childhood, lived in the same town and went to the same schools. Carol was a talented and popular student who went on to university and finally settled down with the love of her life back in our hometown. Their first child Simon arrived a couple of years into the marriage and everything seemed great. All healthy and happy. Her husband Eric had been a wonderful match and was getting the balance right between work as a research scientist and family life. He found his research captivating, following his lifelong interest in energy generation and storage.

Then one day Eric and Simon just disappeared. No explanation and no trace. The police had organised searches and national campaigns. Rewards were offered. They even tried psychics and other more dubious attempts but nothing. Not a clue. It just didn't make any sense. The local gossip alternated between whether they'd deliberately disappeared and Eric had taken his son and gone to start a new life somewhere or they'd been murdered and the bodies successfully disposed of. This was largely malicious and seemed to only be based on the fact that no bodies were found or ransoms demanded. This struck an extra blow as now suspicion moved to my friend Carol.

I didn't believe any of that, but I also couldn't offer any other explanation. The best I could do was just listen when needed and be that shoulder to cry on. It had been getting worse lately and last night was the two-year anniversary of their disappearance. If anniversary is the right word. It implies some sort of celebration.

During the second bottle of red, we played the same game we'd played regularly since then. WTF happened? What'd we miss?

What did the police miss? Did the psychics babble actually contain a clue? And on it went. Over and over.

Then she moved onto the what-ifs. What if she hadn't gone to work that day? What if she hadn't stopped for groceries… Sherlock Holmes said to Dr. Watson "How often have I said to you that when you have eliminated the impossible, whatever remains, however improbable, must be the truth?" This rewording of Ockham's razor was a point we'd reached regularly but never seemed to satisfy ourselves that we'd eliminated the impossible to understand what was left.

Tonight we reached a new low and at the time it made sense. We'd eliminated everything sensible and this was all that was left. Somehow Eric's research project had done something and had either destroyed them both or transported them somewhere or something equally sci-fi. This seemed like a much better idea as we started the third bottle of red. There was a clarity of thought and boldness in action that our desperation convinced us to try.

The police had looked at all of Eric's equipment and called in the university to see if they could explain what it was for. They couldn't. It didn't seem to be related to anything that was a cohesive project. Just lots of seemingly unrelated equipment. It was all still as it had been left. Each piece had been checked, evaluated and then returned to its original place and settings. We plugged in everything we could find and turned it all on.

Nothing happened.

This wasn't that big a surprise but we were disappointed anyway. As we sat staring at the equipment, we noticed a faint shimmering in the centre of the room. It was a bit like a heat mirage. We stared at it for a while trying to make sure that it wasn't just a consequence of the wine. Carol got up from her chair, staggered towards it and disappeared! I was suddenly a lot more sober and starting to freak out.

WTF!

| 2 |

Countdown

Where did she go?

As I looked around the room in disbelief, I noticed what I'd thought was a clock counting down.

09:22
09:21
09:20

Was that something to do with it? I stared at the numbers trying to imagine what they meant. A 10-minute countdown? To what? I found I was stuck in the chair. I couldn't move. My heart rate had jumped enormously and my fight or flight reflexes seemed to have deserted me as I sat paralysed with fear and indecision. Neither leg would respond to instruction. Was Carol dead? This sort of shit just does not happen.

In an alcohol haze and with blood and hormones pumping like they'd never pumped before, I tried to think. I tried to rewind recent events. What exactly was the nature of Eric's research? At different times, it'd come up in conversations. Mostly a bit of teasing Eric about being a mad professor type. A bit Doc Brown and a bit Honey I shrunk the Kids.

Oh no. What if it had shrunk her? I really shouldn't move just in case. What if it was time travel? I was really wishing that I'd paid more attention. I couldn't remember anything about flux capacitors, so it probably wasn't time travel. I also couldn't remember anything about shrinking anything or any Hank Pym references. Had my best friend since childhood just died?

06:15
06:14

The only thing I could think of was to wait until the countdown stopped and see what happened next. As I waited, it occurred to me that the countdown timer might have nothing to do with what had happened at all and was just a consequence of turning on everything we could find. The more I thought about the options the more terrified I became. What if it's a bomb?

03:29
03:28
03:27

I was now just staring at the numbers. Hypnotised by the seconds reducing. Realising that I was holding my breath, I struggled to regain enough composure to exhale like a burst balloon and take in some air. The sound reverberated so loudly in the quiet of the basement workshop that it scared me again making my heart leap wildly. I couldn't take much more of this. I watched the countdown timer reach the final minute.

01:00
00:59
00:58

I couldn't take my eyes from the display. Was I about to die? Should I turn it off before it reaches zero? Could I do it, even if I wanted to.

00:36
00:35
00:34

I couldn't move. That seemed to answer that. I couldn't even if I wanted to. I was too scared.

00:15
00:14

A movement in the centre of the room caught my eye as what looked like a screwed-up piece of paper just appeared from the shimmer and fell to the floor. I heard myself exhale an incoherent uhh???

00:09
00:08

Suddenly out of the shimmer Carol appeared to step back into the room. Everything started to spin and then went dark. I think I passed out.

| 3 |

Carols

Two Carols

As I came to, Carol was shaking me.

"What happened?" we both said at the same time.

I said, "You just disappeared for 10 minutes and then came back out of nowhere."

"I went to the future" said Carol.

"You what!"

"Something terrible is going to happen in the future... Look!" Carol held out her phone and I tried to focus on the screen.

"What am I looking at?" I asked. "I'm just so happy you aren't dead and neither am I. We aren't are we?"

"Look at the screen" insisted Carol.

I poked myself in the leg. It felt real. I poked her in the arm. That felt real too. Good!

"What is it?" I asked.

"It's a huge message written in the sky.
Asteroids to strike Earth in two weeks - Confirmed!"

"What does it mean?" I asked again, "Where did you go?" I could feel my heart rate starting to jump through the roof again.

Ignoring my question, Carol declared "We have to do something".

I looked in disbelief as another person entered the room.

"Who are you?" Carol and I said together. They didn't say anything, just looked at us. As I studied the person's face, and the eyes, I realised it was my friend Carol, the one standing beside me but older. My jaw dropped and I started to sway. The older version of my friend smiled at us and said. "Yep, it's me".

| **4** |

The older Carol explains

A trip back in time

Carol and I stared in silence as words and thoughts tried to gather into coherence. It wasn't working. I vaguely remember mumbling incoherently and making goldfish impressions as our mouths opened and closed without any words forming. The stranger was clearly my friend but older. We both knew her mum, sisters and cousins and she wasn't any of them.

"Yes, it's me. It's so good to see you again" staring straight at me. She marched directly towards me and hugged me like a dear and long-lost friend.

"Wendy, I've missed you so much. I went back in time 20 years."

Carol and I both exploded… "You what!"

"I know this has just happened for you but 20 years has gone by for me. Let me explain."

We sat in numb silence, staring in disbelief.

"As I stepped into the centre of the room I suddenly found myself in this room but it was different. None of the equipment was here and to me, you'd just vanished. I was sobering up very quickly and ran up the stairs to find the house empty. Also it was daylight. Bright daylight. I was trying to figure out what on Earth had happened when I saw a newspaper on the lawn of the house next door. Grabbing it and opening it showed the date as 20 years ago. I was completely stunned."

"My mind was going a thousand miles an hour as I started to dimly see what had happened to Eric and Simon. They were probably not dead or had deliberately gone missing but had gone through the same experience. I realised that if exactly the same thing that happened to me had happened to them, they would've appeared 22 years before I left the present. Where would they've gone? I realised they'd have been stuck in the past. I decided that my best option was to stay in the past and try finding them or at least preventing them from going back without me."

"I wasn't really sober and the elation I was feeling at the idea that they may still be alive was intoxicating. I resolved to stay and search for them. All this had happened in less than 5 minutes. I raced back inside and scribbled a quick note and threw it back into the shimmering thing just before it disappeared. That's it there on the floor. I sent that back 20 years ago when I decided to stay in the past and prepare." She bent down, picked up the paper and passed it to me. "I did go a bit Sarah Connor" she said almost sheepishly.

I unscrunched the scrap of paper and read in a messy scrawl.

I'm OK.

Gone back in time 20 years. Don't know how.

Eric and Simon must be here too. Will look for them.

Thank you and love always. XXX

There was a strange silence as we looked at each other intently.

"Are you me?" asked my friend Carol to the older woman.

"Yes. A 20-year older version."

"How is that possible?" Carol asked incredulously.

"Did you find them?" I asked, ignoring her question.

"Yes and I understand more about what happened to them. It was an accident. A complete bloody accident. Simon accidentally fell into the time shimmer thing and disappeared before Eric's eyes. In horror, he realised what had happened and in an attempt to get Simon back had followed. The problem is that the device wasn't ready. It didn't send them back 20 years but at least 40 years. I still don't understand why but there's a randomness to it. It has something to do with the amount of power available at the time it's used."

"It took me some years to get to this understanding and so I began to prepare to prevent the moment that they first went through. I couldn't. It still happened. Maybe there's some universal law that stopped me. I really don't know. Anyway, the fact that you went to the future is one of the missing parts of the puzzle. I'd been told that's how it works but it seemed too outrageous to be true.

I thought that the universe would prevent things like this. Apparently it doesn't care. The device creates a time bubble, like a sphere but in more than 3 dimensions. At the point where I went through I simultaneously went to the extremity of the bubble in every direction."

"You mean I went forward and backward at the same time" suggested younger Carol.

"Sort of. I'll need to process this myself but I think that's way too simplistic. I think that I not only went forward and backward but also every which ways of sideways."

"I don't know what that means?" Carol and I said at the same time.

"Okay Carol, I really need to know what happened when you went to the future. Tell me every detail."

| 5 |

Carol in the future

Asteroid warning

I watched as Carol tried to gather her thoughts, still reeling from the explanation. "Hang on", she reached over and tentatively pushed her finger into the older woman's arm. "Sorry, I had to do that" she apologised.

"Uhh... okay."

"As you'd remember we were pretty smashed when we thought it was a good idea to try this. I remember sort of falling into the shimmery thing and hitting the floor. The first thing I noticed was that it was suddenly bright daylight. As I looked around, everything had gone. The lab, Wendy and the furniture were all gone. The house seemed empty and dusty and had an old musty smell. I got up and looked outside. The street was different. Mr Henderson's house wasn't there. Suddenly I was hyper alert. What on Earth was going on? I walked to the front door and onto the porch. That's when I looked up at the sky. Written in huge letters across the blue sky was the message. I grabbed my phone and took a picture. Here. Take a look."

She handed over the phone to herself. I realised I was holding my breath again. I think I was waiting for one of them to disappear or explode or something.

"Mmm. Okay. What then?"

"I was shocked and awed. My mind was reeling. Was this true? A movie stunt? Was it real? Just then the message was replaced by a newsreader or something like that. They were talking but I couldn't hear what they were saying. My eyes were glued to the bottom right of the image which showed the date. 20 years in the future. Jan 2039. I didn't get a picture of that. I was shitting bricks and getting the hell out of there. I ran back to the house and straight back into the shimmery thing and I was back here."

"We must go to the authorities; we really need some help with this" said the older Carol.

I felt my friend bristle at the older woman's commanding firm control of the situation. I thought, uh-oh, this is getting even weirder. I don't think Carol likes this woman and this woman is her. That doesn't bode well.

| 6 |

The briefing

The Carver Device and is the asteroid a real threat?

Captain Miller flicked a switch, returning the room to light and the screen to the dark background of the Protectors logo.

"And that people, is our best reconstruction of what actually happened. It was put together after interviews with the three women, two of whom were co-operative. It's a mess. No two ways about it. They had no idea what they were doing and in grief and desperation did something really foolish."

"The upshot of all this is that Carol's husband, Eric Carver may be the greatest genius to have ever lived... or not, considering he was trying to create an energy source and instead created a time portal device. For the philosophers amongst you, should it still be called genius if someone invents or discovers something accidentally and doesn't know what they've done. I'm thinking of ones like Penzias and Wilson with the Cosmic Background Radiation (CBR). You know, people who accidentally found something, didn't know what it was but it turned out to be a really important step forward for humanity and they still got the credit anyway."

"Anyway, I was in the first team to investigate. Both the younger women were totally freaked out and babbled out everything that happened and as you can see from that video, they could remember a lot of detail. This version is from the perspective of Wendy, the one we now call 'The Controller'. More on her later. They made contact with authorities in Australia who handed them over to us and we took the equipment and began a serious study."

"This is what we know so far. It turns out it's possible to move in time in both directions. It requires more power to go further from now in either direction. Lots and lots of power. Lots more than the 1.21 gigawatts of electricity Doc Brown needed to send Marty back to the future."

"The problem of creating multiple copies of a person was identified and is now solved. As far as we know, the multiple copies problem only applies to the Carver family."

"A team was assembled, led by the highly respected and decorated Col. Zac Armstrong and sent to investigate. The first question we felt had to be answered was about the asteroids. Was it true? We had experts check Carol's phone and it appeared to be completely legitimate. There was no disruption of her phone internally. We could see the moment her phone stopped talking to the network and when it reconnected. In between, the logs clearly show, it tried to connect and couldn't. Also the photo was forensically analysed and there's no faking. It's genuine."

"So, we were faced with the question. Is the Earth really going to be hit by asteroids in 20 years time? Should we be worried? In the security services we prefer the rephrasing, 'How worried should we be?' And that's exactly what we wanted to know."

"I've concluded that people in general have trouble dealing with this amount of disruption to their understanding of time, space and the universe, which is why it's helpful to break it down into more manageable chunks."

"On a lighter note, I found that we each tend to have a particular phrase or expression that we use when we're told things like this. When I went through it, my involuntary expression of incredulity was - *You've got to be shitting me.* There were some small variations, like FFS, you've got to be shitting me and the occasional 'Ho-ly Sh-it!', expressed as four well-articulated and distinct syllables."

"I know at this stage you may think it's a strange thing to talk about, but I'll mention this again at the end of the day and we'll see what you think then. Be aware, the staff are running a book on your reactions and the most popular expressions of incredulity in today's sessions may well be immortalised."

"Now, I know that many of you are now fighting internal battles as various pillars that supported your understanding of the universe have just been kicked out from under you. I'll explain further after you see this next video. This presentation was put together from the evidence of some survivors of the asteroids. Be forewarned, it's confronting."

"Also, I'm showing you the information as it presented itself to us, with some broader perspectives added when relevant. Please keep track of how many times you blurt out your favourite expletive, involuntary expression or sound. Let's get started."

| 7 |

Mission One

After the Asteroids

Captain Miller began, "As this was our first mission, we weren't certain that we could hit a point in the future exactly. The margin of error was still large. We didn't have good control over the accuracy of the device. It was measured in years at that stage, so it was decided to include that margin after the asteroid was due to strike. This meant up to three years after. We were lucky, in a way, as Col. Armstrong's team arrived about 9 months after the date mentioned in Carol's video. That first time through the lens was not good. Actually, it was devastating for everyone involved. Asteroids did strike and it destroyed our civilization."

"Col. Armstrong's team made contact with some survivors and they barely escaped with their lives. The survivors weren't happy. They were starving and scared witless as anarchy had taken over. Communication even over short distances was disrupted which made the team's ability to spread out difficult. One group of survivors they met really wanted to go with Col. Armstong. They thought they'd come to rescue them. In the skirmish that broke out we had our first casualty. Captain Johnson. This is the actual video taken by Col. Armstrong during that mission."

He waved at a technician at the back of the room who started the video. The large screen at the front of the room came to life and showed a man who had obviously been through a rough time. You could see that he'd been a handsome man but now…

He looked into the camera and said in a slow, deliberate voice, "We knew about the asteroids. Lots of objects were tracked just in case one might collide with Earth. The asteroid field was observed 3 years out. We knew an approximate day and time and no one knew quite what to do. There was a lot of wild speculation about where they would hit and where if anywhere, would be safe."

The camera panned away from the man to reveal a terrifying sight. The sky looked like a boiling black cauldron of dangerous looking clouds. It was completely dark with no visible sunlight, stars or moon. You could only see the clouds because colossal sheets of lightning were continuously illuminating the sky behind and around them.

"It didn't work. The cloud of material in the atmosphere blocked out the sun and the plants and animals suffered enormously. Most of them died in the first three months. No crops would grow, solar and wind became useless. These were desperate times."

Captain Miller went on, "The team returned and weren't keen to go back. Apparently the smell was unforgettable. Many of the team had been in disaster areas and war zones before but this was something else. The stench of rotting carbon-based life on a colossal scale."

"Col. Armstrong was unable to get any clear picture of what had happened or where it had impacted. No one seemed to know for sure. Global communications weren't working."

"If that wasn't strange, challenging and confronting enough, the man went on to tell an even stranger story about an event that happened nearly twenty years before the asteroids. And before you ask, he should know, he was the Vice-President of the United States of America at the time. More on that later."

"This next video is a mixture of actual footage, a documentary they brought back and some reconstruction built from what the final Vice-President of the USA told Col. Armstrong." He dimmed the lights once more and said, "Start the video".

| 8 |

Outside the Solar System

The screen flickered and showed senior technician Maya Chandra looking closely at the monitor in front of her in disbelief. The display showed a large group of objects passing through the outer solar system. Not the usual range of sizes from the tiny to the size of an SUV. These were big. Huge.

She called out to her colleague, "Hey Jo, check this out. Something isn't right about this. The trajectories and speeds just don't seem to make sense. Has there been some massive collision in the Oort cloud? The Kuiper Belt? Did Planet X just explode?" She suddenly went rigid as the realisation hit her.

"OMG Jo, these aren't natural objects." The idea that these could be alien craft or operating under alien control was inconceivable but she was running out of options that fitted the data she was seeing.

"I'm seeing at least 1000 objects heading towards the inner solar system and potentially Earth and some of them are big. They both looked at each other as every sci-fi nightmare erupted in their minds at the same time."

"Is it an alien invasion? Who are we supposed to call when you come across information like this? The President? Do Ghost-busters have an alien division? What's the protocol for this? Who would know? She picked up the phone and called her boss Dr Hacker. It was 3am and her boss would be sound asleep. She called him anyway.

Her boss answered grumpily. "What!?"

"It's Maya Chandry, are you sitting down?"

"I'm in bed you idiot. What?"

"You've got to see this" she said, feeling the uneasiness growing in the pit of her stomach.

| 9 |

What can we do about it?

The President looks for options

The crisis management group sat around the oval office, their faces whiter than normal.

"What options do we have?" asked the President.

"We're still gathering information," the NASA administrator declared.

"Okay.... Someone give me some scenarios" demanded the President testily.

"Very well Mr President," Ed Raines, the National Security Advisor began, "Scenario one. The data is really showing something else. There's an error in the analysis. They really are odd asteroids or other space junk. Scenario two. They're aliens, they're hostile, they're coming to Earth and intend to attack us. Scenario 3. They're aliens, they're not hostile, they're coming to Earth and they have some other intention apart from attacking us. Scenario 4. Something completely unknown to us. The 'unknown unknowns' situation."

"Okay," said the President, tilting his head encouragingly, expecting more.

Ed Raines continued, "If we assume they're coming to Earth, and are hostile, what can we do about it? We have no information about their weapons capabilities at all. We can speculate, but we may as well get a bunch of sci-fi writers in here and start making up stuff. Our most powerful weapons are planetary based. If we wanted a pre-emptive strike we would need to get them before they got to Earth but we have no ability to get our weapons to the edge of the solar system in time… or even to Mars or the Moon. Let alone, target and fire them."

"This brings up another consideration. Our best guesstimates of how long before they arrive is between two and three days. Make a note of that. Days. Not weeks or months. Whatever we decide to do, we have to get it right the first time."

A civilian advisor, Dr. Jayne Osborne spoke up, "Ahum… what if they have no hostile intention? What will their reaction be to us firing at them if they're on a diplomatic or research mission… or just out for a joy ride. Do we really need to piss off people we've never met before that have the ability to move between stars?"

"What's our first opportunity to make contact with them?" asked the President.

The chief scientist, Dr. Myron Hathaway, added, "All our communications are based on light speed or less. So we can send a signal to them and get a reply within a few hours. Pretty hard way to talk but it would give us some warning at least."

"Okay" said the President firmly, "Send them a message welcoming them to our solar system and ask about their intentions."

"In what language should we send it?" the NASA administrator asked.

"Everyone you can think of" replied the President, "Let's find out if they'll declare their intentions and in the meantime I want some options in case they turn out to be hostile."

"Do you want to make any public statement yet?" The White House Chief of Staff, Mark Graham was already thinking about damage control. "A number of observatories are already tracking the objects. We can't stop all of them."

"Not yet. Let's not go down that path until we know more" the President said quietly.

| 10 |

Is this for real?

The fleet splits and some head for Europa

Back at the tracking station, Maya Chandra was looking intently at her screen, trying to focus on what she was seeing. The expression on her face showed incredulity. "It doesn't make sense! The objects are splitting up into smaller groups and new objects seem to be appearing from nowhere. It's not possible."

"Oh yes it is" her colleague Jo Wilde retorted, "I'm seeing it too".

"Where did all the new objects just come from? There are three times as many objects as before. How is that possible?" she repeated, "The boss isn't going to like this at all."

Jo called out, "I've been trying to plot the trajectories of the new objects and some seem to be heading for Europa."

Maya confirmed it a few minutes later. She turned to Jo wide eyed and said, "A third of the objects have begun to orbit Europa. The rest have now passed Jupiter and are continuing on to Earth.

"What's on Europa?" Jo wondered.

"Maybe Arthur C Clarke was right about that moon" Maya said. "It's one of the most likely places for LIFE to be, in our solar system. If it hadn't been Europa, I would've guessed Enceladus next."

"Which one of us is going to ring the boss?" asked Maya. "I did it last time. Isn't it your turn?"

"Oh no," Jo said smiling broadly, "that's why they pay you the big bucks, Senior Technician Chandry."

"I know. It has to be me doesn't it," Maya said reluctantly, "I just hate it when he yells at me. I'm just the messenger."

Final minutes before the fleet arrives

The White house Situation Room

Mark Graham, the White House Chief of Staff began his report. "There's been no reply to our messages, Mr President. It's been sent in every human and machine language using audio, video and even sign languages. We've tried all the techniques suggested by our 'experts' in alien contact. Nothing's worked and they're less than four hours away."

"How are our preparations coming along in case they're hostile?"

"We're in a very difficult position here. It's likely that our most powerful weapons will be useless against craft like this. They may even use our own energy against us. There is no data to theorise from."

"So, science fails again eh! Can't deliver when we need it."

"That's a bit harsh Mr President" his senior science advisor admonished.

"Hmmm, we'll see," replied the president.

"We're on high alert and we'll have to respond instantly to the evolving situation. My biggest fear at the moment is that we mess it up ourselves. They turn out to be non-hostile and we or someone does something that makes them hostile. We're not the only ones monitoring all this. The Russians, the Chinese, India, Australia, South America. Any country with deep space telescopes are watching them. Any one of them could mess it up for all of us."

Senior advisor Mike Elliot leaned in conspiratorially, "This has got to be approached globally. We need to speak as one planet. I believe that the initial contact should be made by the UN Secretary General. It's our best hope of putting forward a unified front. It also means if anything goes wrong, you're not the first to be eaten or probed or whatever they want to do to us. You've probably seen Tim Burton's 'Mars Attacks'. We can watch what happens and then act to defend and protect our own interests."

"I see your point," said the President, "get the Secretary General on the phone."

"How are we going to sell it to him?" asked Mike Elliott, the science advisor.

"The usual trick is to make it sound like an honour" said the President.

"Mr President, as they moved past Jupiter towards the inner planets, they split again and again. We are now showing over 10,000 objects of assorted sizes."

A military voice stated flatly, "The countdown shows less than a minute till they enter Earth's orbit." In silence they waited, trying to take in every screen and nuance. Every sense was straining for more information. Were they going to be attacked? Were they going to meet visitors from another world? As the countdown finally reached zero. The large screen showed the objects were right above us.

"If they're hostile then this is an invasion fleet of staggering proportions" said Ed Raines, the national security advisor.

"No message from the fleet and no reply to the messages from Earth" his chief of staff added. They watched in silence until each craft found its own unique orbit.

| 12 |

The message

To panic or not to panic, that is the question

Captain Miller continued, "The message appeared simultaneously on every radio, TV and computer on the planet. It seemed to be in the language of the listener, as it was reported later, that several people in one room heard the same broadcast in different languages, while they listened to the same source, however that works. The message was short, simple and completely unexpected."

"Your planet is about to become uninhabitable. Nearly all life will become extinct. This event will occur in around 30 years time. There is nothing that any human can do to prevent this. We have come to transport the population of the planet to other worlds, in order for your forms of life to survive. The fleet above you is a mixture of volunteers and galactic aid organisations. After this initial contact we will give you one week to prepare for the first evacuation. Because of the amount of LIFE on this planet, we will need to make multiple trips to get every-

one to safety. During the coming week, we will have the opportunity to make contact with individual leaders and to answer some of your immediate questions. We ask that you look to your local leaders for guidance through this initial stage."

"As you might expect, the reaction was quick and intense. Many panicked. Governments and leaders tried to pretend they knew what was going on. 'Don't panic' seemed to be the advice coming from all sides. Douglas Adams would have been so proud. Some even took notice."

"During the first 24 hours, information started to flow. Normal TV had basically ceased as every channel began streaming live events and commentary. The initial public reaction wasn't so much about the content of the message but was more focussed on the fact that there were alien spacecraft above Earth. This caused problems for several groups who had stated categorically that this could never happen. Most now back-pedalled, saying, no we never said that, we said it was unlikely or improbable, in direct contrast to the video and printed evidence."

"They weren't some Galactic army, but a rag tag collection of individuals and groups who had a craft that could be spared to help in the effort. It was more like the evacuations that took place across the English Channel during D-Day. It was a Galactic humanitarian effort. It also became clear that not all the craft were occupied by beings that looked the same as humans. Apparently, they were from a number of different solar systems and represented 5 different races or species. At that stage no one knew how to categorise them."

"They were aware that the number of craft together may have been viewed as hostile, but there was little that could be done about it in the timeframe. When asked about whether they were concerned that someone might take a pot shot at them. They said they were unconcerned about our weapons capabilities. They didn't actually say that we were too primitive to hurt them but it sounded something like that... and we all thought it."

"It also became clear they weren't only concerned about humans. They were intending to relocate all LIFE from Earth or at least a representative sample of all LIFE. This story was starting to sound a bit familiar and they explained that this had been done at least four times before in their recorded history. They'd collected the inhabitants of the planet, the flora and fauna and samples of every rock and element."

"Apparently the distribution of elements on Earth is more important than we humans are aware. A regular Noah's Ark. In fact it may explain the origins of the Noah's Ark story or Utnapishtim from the Epic of Gilgamesh or Manu from the Vedic legends."

| 13 |

Lots of questions

An alternative view

The President had just finished a prolonged rant about the SETI program, the Search for Extraterrestrial Intelligence. He'd said loudly and repeatedly, "I blame SETI and all the crap we broadcast into space. How did the aliens know about us? How did they know where we were? I always thought SETI was a bad idea. It's like chickens trying to attract the attention of foxes, in the belief that not all foxes are chicken-killers. There's bound to be some good foxes out there somewhere. We just have to hope we don't attract the wrong sort."

"Why should we believe them?" the President spat into his coffee. This disrupted his diatribe as he noticed the unsavoury floaty bits. He raised his glowering gaze back to the assembled group of advisors and continued gesticulating inarticulately.

"How do we know we can trust them? How can we even believe our own senses after that telepathy message thing? General, what does the military think?"

General Emmerson said, "We shouldn't be taken in by this deception. We need concrete proof that the events they describe will happen and that there's nothing we can do about it. We must. We can't just take their word that we have to abandon our civilization and flee. Humans have been so resilient in the past, why not now. What makes this so much different?"

"So many questions and so little time to ask them" said the president returning to inarticulate gesticulation, "What are the other worlds like? Will we be free, slaves... refugees? Can we transfer wealth and power? Who'll own the animal and plant materials that are gathered. Will humans have any say in how they're used or by whom or for what?"

"Does our law just get thrown away?" chipped in Mark Graham, the White House Chief of Staff.

"Okay, I get it. The consequences are huge. Any other views before we get to options?" demanded the President.

"How about trying to get hold of one of those craft for ourselves?" suggested General Emmerson.

"Thoughts?"

"How about... we don't know how to fly it. Or fuel it. Or if they can blow it up remotely?" said Mark Graham.

"What about trying to attack one of the craft and blame it on someone else? To see what their offensive capabilities are like. We've used that tactic successfully in the past" said General Emmerson.

"You want to attempt to deceive beings who've demonstrated the ability to telepathically contact every human on the planet simultaneously. Even God doesn't do that or hasn't for a long time" the Chief of Staff added dryly, "We have a series of unanswered questions that need to be answered. I've narrowed it down to broad categories. What will happen to the Earth, humanity and human civilization and what does this setup for the future?"

The Chief of Staff consulted his notes. "In no particular order... firstly, what is the exact nature of the disaster about to befall Earth? Where is the proof that the event they're describing will actually happen? If it's true, how do we dismantle part of our civilization in a week and for the rest to stay put and do whatever they normally do to keep everything running. Do we need to consider martial law?"

"Secondly, what will happen to humanity? Is humanity about to be absorbed into a larger group of beings, of which only some are human? Is this cosmic multiculturalism? Are there other human colonies out there? Are we all going to the same planet? Will we ever be able to come back to Earth?"

"And finally what happens to the people who don't want to go? Will all the people be evacuated or will it only be some? If we have to go, what do we take with us? What status will we have? Will we be considered refugees? How will we know they've arrived safely? ...and on it goes. We've put together some experts who have contrasting views to help you reach a conclusion or at least a strategy we can live with."

"Can we get one of the alien leaders to talk to us and answer these questions?" the President asked, nearly rhetorically, "Has anyone got a line to them? Who would we talk to?"

"At this stage all communications are being channelled through the UN," the Chief of Staff said, "we can try and set something up."

"Do it. Let's get some real data. Some actual facts."

An alien view of Earth's history

The ISS and the astronauts become chess pieces

Mark Graham sat across from the President and shuffled his notes. "Mr President, the UN granted us access to a spokesperson for the fleet. All their communication so far has been with this one individual. No one has seen him and they talk only, no visuals. We have no idea whether he is human or human-like or whether any of our genders apply but the general view is that we're hearing a masculine voice."

"Do we have any idea what he looks like?" asked the President.

"No. When he speaks it appears he speaks English but another staff member who was present said they heard the replies in Tagalog, his first language. Nobody has any idea how that works."

The President looked mystified, "Okay, what have you learnt?"

"Apparently it's the custom amongst the aliens who participate in these rescues to impart knowledge to those who decide to stay behind. The UN has shared the data they received. It's very detailed and includes Earth observations for the last 100,000 odd years including the last three precession cycles. The data itself is pretty amazing. They've been watching remotely the whole time. Maybe some variation of the Black Knight Satellite. It also seems their communications aren't instantaneous. There is a time lag."

"The basic thesis is that our Earth revolves around the Sun. Our Sun revolves around the Milky Way's galactic centre. It takes one year for the Earth to go round the Sun. It takes the Sun 225 - 250 million years to go around the galactic centre while the Earth wobbles in a 26,000-year cycle known as precession."

"As our solar system moves through its galactic orbit, it's bathed periodically in peculiar combinations of radiation, gravitational forces and asteroid belts which makes it a very poor supporter of LIFE. Various objects shield us and then move away, or we move away and get the full blast from clusters of pulsars and other things that give off huge amounts of energy or create gravity effects. Depending on the mixture of LIFE on the planet when that happens, it's either disastrous or catastrophic. If this is combined with another LIFE threatening event like massive geological or volcanic activity, extinctions happen on a grand scale."

"The evacuations of previous generations were recorded by the peoples left behind and became a mixture of legend, allegory and bullshit. The difference this time is the population of the Earth is so much larger. Apparently by giving information to the ones who remain, it increases the chances of LIFE returning more quickly."

"The alien we spoke with seemed disappointed that some animals were now extinct. Sounded like he had a few favourites. Some information survived from the last time and was maintained by various cultures. A possible explanation for the seemingly unknowable mathematics, astronomy and engineering that seemed to arrive in history intact. It mightn't explain everything, but it may explain a bit. Some of the astronomical information was about where the refugees were going."

"So, the threat to the planet is real. What about the rest?" asked the President.

We struggled with the right language, to make sure 'he' understood what a refugee was. I'm still not certain we mean the same thing. It was hard to get him to talk about this. He seemed very unconcerned. I personally believe it means exactly what we think. The people will be refugees and unable to transfer wealth, power or status, except amongst our own people. He seems to struggle with ideas like property and ownership, particularly of planetary land. "

"Does he want us to organise ourselves?" asked the President.

"I believe that's the case. At least to organise people to board the ships, behave, maintain peace etc."

"Do we know who he represents? What type of political structure operates?" the President asked.

"Not exactly but we did learn a bit about the political system. For a start there are many civilisations out there. The Drake equation puts it somewhere between 'a few and millions', which is so broad as to be useless." While there are variations on Republics, Monarchies and Oligarchies, this mission isn't organised by them. This is more about average citizens doing their bit for LIFE. A bit like a volunteer relief organisation. They aren't a cohesive group from one civilisation, more like concerned citizens."

"Do you believe him?" the President asked sceptically.

"Truthfully, I have no idea. It seems like an unusual lie if it's a lie."

"What about our laws?"

"Again, it's hard to keep him on that topic as he doesn't seem to understand why it's important to us."

The President took a deep breath and looked off into the distance.

"So, I have to make a decision based on little information, most of which can't be confirmed and I have to do it within 72 hours."

"Okay, I want better information. We'll encourage our people to go along with the alien's proposal while we get other, better intelligence. I want something at least as good as the justification of the Invasion of Iraq, if not better." He dismissed the meeting and watched them file out. He poured himself and his Chief of Staff large whiskies, sat at his desk and began to sip appreciatively.

"You know what keeps bugging me Mark. I keep coming back to the same question. Why did no one come back? Surely whatever was out there, wasn't so absorbing that not even a single person wanted to come back to Earth... ever? That single question kept me awake last night. Why hasn't a single person ever come back? I can't believe that no one would want to. Human curiosity should guarantee that someone would. It makes me uneasy. Why hadn't they? Something's not right. How can we get on one of those ships? We need to see what's in those ships. "

His Chief of Staff pondered as he slowly sipped his whisky. "What if we simulate an accident in space? We could ask for help to pick up our stranded astronauts. They'll be able to get into position much quicker than we can. Once on board, our astronauts will get the first glimpse of the technologies we're dealing with. At the very least, we could get some ideas about their technology. Is it based on light, heat, radiation, or something else completely? How is power generated? Do they have weapons, how do they work?"

"What do you think?

The President mulled it over, swilling the whisky in a steady circular motion, "Make a plan. We'll talk about it tomorrow."

| 15 |

A bold plan

Desperate times calls for desperate measures

The next morning, the crisis management response team met again. No one looked like they'd slept much. When they'd settled into their seats, General Emmerson took the floor.

"Mr President, we've developed a plan along the lines you requested. In order for it to be as realistic as possible we've prepared scenarios where we create or cause an explosion aboard the International Space Station, maybe even losing an astronaut or two to avoid any doubt that it's an uncontrolled accident."

"The idea is to make the ISS uninhabitable in some way. The more spectacular the better and then request that one of the craft pick up the stranded astronauts or they'll die. If we take out the life support system then the astronauts will be on a countdown that's easily measurable based on how much air they've got left. We've identified a way of taking out major components of life support and the two Soyuz capsules designated as the emergency escape vehicles, so they have no choice. If they don't intervene on our behalf then the astronauts will die. I can't deny there are many ways this could go wrong and it could destroy one of our best assets in space."

"How long will it take to put into action?" asked the President, "and what's the likelihood that they'd ignore our request for assistance or have some plausible reason why they can't help?"

"Unknowable at the moment but in the spirit of cooperation they may be convinced. The NASA administrator would probably beg. Mr President, we're about to find out if they'll negotiate about anything or demonstrate empathy or…"

The President cut him off, "Would the ISS be recoverable from the damage?"

"Certainly. Of course our guys wanted to do the least amount of damage to our section and most to be in the Russian part. Personally I don't agree. We'd need to suffer some loss too."

"In three days' time, on Wednesday morning, a Soyuz mission is due to dock with the ISS. We could time an explosion just as the resupply capsule is about to dock. The explosion could move the ISS at a critical stage of the docking process causing the capsule to crash into the main structure doing enough damage to create the crisis."

"We would then go through our normal procedures, done through Mission Control, who will eventually realise that the environment isn't sustainable and the remaining astronauts will die unless something else happens. Mission Control will escalate the situation to us and we'll contact the alien fleet leader to apprise them of the situation and ask if there's any way they could help us. The panic from the crew and Mission Control will be genuine and sincere and of course the astronauts will want to live."

"What is the current crew of the ISS?"

"There are seven crew aboard led by Commander Epsom and they're due to return seven days after the Soyuz capsule docks. About ten days from now."

"How could it go wrong?" asked the President, "speak plainly."

"As you said, the aliens might ignore or refuse the request. The explosion may do more damage than we hope or not enough. Very hard to judge and we'd have to go for more rather than less, to make sure that it worked. We're still refining the plan to improve the likelihood of success."

"Hmmm," the President looked determined. "Do it."

| 16 |

The Day of the explosion

Commander Sally Epsom woke and felt that rush again. I'm in space and on the International Space Station. I love my life. She unstrapped herself, floated out of her sleeping bag and towards the Node 3 workout zone. She was thinking about her exercise routine and the day ahead when suddenly, a noise boomed and vibrated through the station as a series of alarms went off. She recognised fire, pressure loss and system malfunction alarms as they became a cacophony of audible pandemonium.

"What was that?" she yelled over the noise, "Mission Control, what just happened? Have we been hit?"

"Commander Epsom, an object has struck the Ros and destroyed part of it, at least" said Mission Control, "there were at least two people in the module when this occurred. We've lost their bioinstrumentation and stopped receiving video signals. We have some telemetry but no visuals so we're operating partially blind down here. At least one of you needs to get to the Cupola and see what you can see."

Commander Epsom floated in the direction of the big bay window meeting mission specialist Dr Emoto along the way. He was the current Kibo laboratory and robotic arm expert.

"I'm heading to the Cupola for a better view. Mission Control isn't getting any video feeds."

"I heard", said Dr Emoto, floating towards her. As they approached the Cupola, they found payload specialist Dr Asimov was already there and had started opening the seven window covers. This always takes a few minutes.

"I can see there's damage to some of the solar panels and there seems to be more debris than I can see damage" Commander Epsom reported to Mission Control.

"How many crew members have you been in contact with?" asked Mission Control.

"There are three of us at the Cupola and we've had no contact with the other four."

"Someone will need to go outside to assess the damage" said Mission Control. "We're showing that the Russian section automatically sealed itself and to the best of our knowledge there were four people in that section. We've lost their telemetry."

Over the next hour, a new picture started to emerge. An unidentified object had struck the ISS somewhere around the Russian modules Zarya and Zvezda which had caused a rapid depressurisation and so the modules sealed themselves. It was still unclear whether any of those four crew members survived.

Commander Epsom had clocked up 42 hours spacewalking which made her the most experienced at EVAs and so she suited up in the Quest airlock in the Harmony module.

Once through the airlock, she started following the network of handrails and foot holds to get a clearer view. As she cleared the top of the module, her heart stopped. There was stuff everywhere. The Zarya and Zvezda modules were in tatters with enormous holes in the sides. Various storage items were floating around and then she saw the first body. It must be Flight specialist Ivor Tunny but he'd been cut in two and the two halves of the body were floating apart.

"OMG!"

She snapped a series of still images and then to her horror another object struck the station straight through the Cupola section. And just like that she was alone. Outside the remains of the station and uncertain whether anyone of her crew remained.

"Mission Control, did you just see any of that? The Cupola's been destroyed. I saw Dr Asimov sucked out into space but I didn't see Dr Emoto."

"My God."

"This is Mission Control; we want you to re-enter the airlock and wait for further instructions." The Mission Control centre was going crazy. What had happened? Had they just lost 6 astronauts? It appeared that the commander was the only one still alive because she was suited up and outside the station.

"What're our options?" called out the Flight Director. "Losing the Russian modules means we've lost our ability to fly the station as well as many communication systems. As far as I can see there are still three modules that can definitely be pressurised and have life support systems. It will take a little while to work out which systems are still operational."

"Where's our resupply mission?"

"It's not due to leave for another 24 hours. We're going to have to scrub that mission."

"Wake up the Administrator, we have a full-blown crisis on our hands. How are we going to save Commander Epsom?"

| 17 |

The response

"Mr President, the NASA administrator has just called to say that there's been a serious explosion or collision with an object that has destroyed much of the International Space Station. It's feared that we've lost all of the crew except for Commander Epsom who was outside the station when the second object hit. They want us to ask one of the alien craft to save her. It's believed that she only has a day or so of oxygen left. She's back inside one of the few remaining modules that can be pressurised but without the aliens' intervention, it appears we'll lose her."

"Can we see what's going on up there?"

"We're moving one of our spy satellites to look at and track the ISS. We should have imagery in a few minutes."

"Arrange for NASA to be able to communicate directly with the alien fleet leader. They'll probably want Commander Epsom to leave the ISS in order to board their craft." Within minutes, they could see the ISS on the monitor. It wasn't in good shape. There was a lot of floating debris and some of the modules were particularly damaged with visible holes and various small objects floating around. A strange looking craft came into view moving in a different way than our spacecraft did. It crawled rather than slid. A message arrived from the alien ship.

There is a lot of debris that we would like to avoid. This is as close as we would like to get to protect our own craft. We will need your stranded astronaut to leave the structure and navigate to the other craft. Can the astronaut propel herself from one craft to the other?

The NASA administrator chimed in with "That is a no. She doesn't have access to that equipment."

She will need to push off from the station and drift to the craft.

"How far away is the ship?"

About 1000 metres.

"That's a fair way untethered and just floating unattached in space."

We can't see any other way.

"Okay. We'll tell Commander Epsom the plan and cross our fingers."

| 18 |

Rescue

Into the abyss

Capt. Miller stood up and said, "This next section is narrated by Commander Epsom herself. It was part of a documentary the team brought back."

The video showed Commander Epsom in the airlock. Her clear voice continued the narration.

"I was quietly waiting for instructions and trying to calm my mind. The NASA flight director talked me through the plan. I was going to get picked up by aliens? This weird and terrible day sounded like it was going to get a lot weirder. I put the deaths of my fellow astronauts out of my mind. I'll grieve for them when I can. Right now, my focus is staying alive."

The radio crackled over the beeps of the quindar tones and Mission Control said, "We're not sure about the life support available on the craft. We think it best if you prepare to keep your suit on for as long as possible".

I forced myself to go slowly as I started to check my EVA suit. I'd put on my 'long johns' or Liquid Cooling and Ventilation Garment and hooked up the various flexible hoses and tubing for the initial EVA. I'd worked through the Prebreathe Protocol to reduce the amount of nitrogen in my body which would prevent decompression sickness while I was outside. I checked the suit's oxygen supply, CO_2 scrubbers and Bio Sensors, finally checking comms by reporting to Mission Control, "I'm as ready as I'm going to be."

"Okay Commander, good luck from everybody here. You may get a new record out of this."

"Not really thinking about that at the moment, Control. Is the alien ship ready?"

"They've indicated they are Commander, you're clear to go."

"The airlock was already closed behind me and had been depressurised. One final check of my suit and I started the process of unlocking and opening the outer hatch."

"I knew the importance of controlling fear and maintaining composure. The idea of leaving the safety of the ISS and pushing off into the void of space untethered was my worst nightmare. Drifting off into the vastness of space, feeling the enormity of the cosmos and the fragility of my existence. To feel total isolation."

"Memories of my training, of emergency procedures, surged to the surface. In the silence, my own bodily sounds and the mechanical hums, clicks and whooshes were a constant reminder of the complex technology keeping me alive in the harsh reality of space."

"I struggled to calm my body while it screamed at me. This was the nightmare I'd had many times as a child. To wake up in deep space in a spacesuit with no other life or object anywhere nearby. In the dream I could feel the incredible distance I was from anything and the growing hopelessness of being rescued. This recurring nightmare had woken me many times during my teens. Dripping in sweat and screaming I'd find my parents in my room talking gently to me as they tried to help me through the night terrors. It always felt so real and so terrifying. Going into the space sciences had been a way of dealing with my fear head on."

"I knew the risk I was taking. In zero gravity every movement becomes a slow ballet as ordinary actions become a challenge. No astronaut had ever done anything like this before. No physical connection to the ISS. No backup life support. I'd trained on the SAFER system (Simplified Aid for EVA Rescue) and it was always talked about as the absolutely last resort. Never be completely untethered."

"I stood at the airlock looking out at the cosmic darkness, the primal roar of adrenaline barely masking the feeling of absolute terror. With a confusing mix of awe and trepidation I pushed off from the ISS airlock hatch into the abyss aiming at the glowing area towards the rear of the alien craft that was some form of airlock, propelled initially by sheer desperation. The Earth, that vibrant blue marble, hung below me, impossibly huge and close, yet so far away."

"The chaotic symphony of alarms were now muted. Reflecting in my visor shield and the special strategically placed mirrors used for looking behind me, emergency lights were flickering as the faint red and orange glow of flames popped up sporadically all over the ISS hull and were then snuffed out from lack of oxygen.

Time lost meaning as every second became an eternity. Who or what was on the other side? Am I about to die? Will I drift forever? What will the aliens be like? I fought to keep my breathing regular and my thoughts in check."

"Amidst the existential terror, a strange peace began to settle. I felt a connection to the universe, a oneness with the cosmos I'd never experienced or imagined before. Instead of being an observer of space, I'd become part of it. I was like the Earth, the Moon and the Sun… an object in space."

"I was trying very hard not to think about the crew I couldn't save or my childhood nightmares or the randomness of the debris as the alien ship slowly loomed larger, glinting in the Earthshine. It was big. Maybe Firefly-class size. I estimated it was 80 metres long. Its unusual design and ethereal glow provided a stark contrast to the darkness of space."

"As fear gave way to sheer determination, I activated the radio, my voice raspy, yet filled with resolve. Control, I'm more than halfway to the rescue craft but I'm not aligned with the airlock. I'll use the SAFER booster to adjust."

"Okay EVA-1, you're doing great. We're monitoring your vitals and levels and everything looks good from here. In a few moments the airlock will open for you. Just head towards the light."

"I engaged the joystick controller for the SAFER system and nudged forward making small adjustments. Towards the back of the ship a light brightened and a small space opened, shining a welcoming light that beckoned me forward as the alien craft grew larger and larger."

"With a final burst of concentration and strength, I reached out and my gloved hand connected with the side of the alien vessel. Manoeuvring awkwardly to deal with my inertia, my feet luckily found a solid surface. The tactile sensation of grabbing onto a foreign surface after the emptiness of space brought a tidal wave of emotions. Relief washed over me. The feeling was even stronger than the first time I'd ridden a rocket into space."

"I'm here. Control, I've made it. I'm inside the airlock. Thank God! Thank you Control. Thank you everyone. Thank you to the designers of the SAFER system. It worked beautifully."

"Congratulations Commander Epsom, you've just made the history books again."

"I went silent trying to manage my breathing and impulses while dealing with a kaleidoscope of emotions." I whispered, "Control, what happens now?"

"Before they could reply the outer wall closed behind me and I was instantly claustrophobic. A warm, soft light enveloped me and as the light increased in brightness, I felt weight returning. I was no longer weightless. This incredible feeling was overwhelmed by a single thought that filled my mind. I'm alive! The universe, for all its vastness and terror, had given me a second chance."

The internal side of the airlock walls dissolved revealing a large cargo bay. A humanoid figure stepped forward. He appeared to be a healthy human male, about 35 years old.

"Welcome Commander Epsom, I am Selec."

"His lips didn't move but the words formed in my mind. In a soothing tone, he assured me that I was safe. The voice had an odd familiarity to it, with traces of a human emotion and warmth that felt like someone I knew."

"Thank you for rescuing me" I said out loud.

"You are welcome. You may remove your suit. The environment has been stabilised to suit humans in every way. It is perfectly safe. The gravity is set to a comfortable .38 of Earth. It's normal for Mars. It will help you transition from weightlessness back to Earth gravity. Would you like assistance removing your suit?"

I knew I had to trust him. He'd just rescued me. "Thank you, that would be a great help."

In minutes I was out of the suit and standing in my slippers and socks on the surprisingly warm floor of the cargo bay.

"It will take about an hour to return you to Earth. Where do you want to be dropped off?" asked Selec.

"Can I communicate with Mission Control? I seem to have lost contact with them since I came on board."

"That is the outer layer of the ship. It doesn't allow random electromagnetic radiation to enter. One moment while I establish a connection." Selec's expression didn't change and nothing seemed to happen for a few seconds. "Speak now and they will hear you."

"Mission Control, this is Commander Sally Epsom. I am safely inside the rescue ship."

"Great to hear from you Commander. We were getting concerned when the radio stopped working so suddenly."

"The outer shell of the ship doesn't pass random EMR. I'm with my rescuer Selec in a large empty cargo space. I've removed my suit and it's beautiful and warm. It's amazing. It's like being in a ballroom-sized room in space and there's a light gravity. It feels incredibly normal. Selec has asked where I want to be taken. What do you suggest?"

"We would prefer you come back to Florida for medical assessment but the powers that be want you to head straight for Washington or as close as you can get. There are some very influential people who want to meet you. We just need to know how long it will take and whether Selec needs a certain size parking space or any other special requirements."

Selec introduced himself to mission control. "Greetings, I am Selec. It will take an hour to leave our current position and go to Washington. I do not require any special parking considerations as I will not actually land on the Earth."

Mission control was silent for a brief moment as they digested that information.

"Okay... would you like us to give you a location?"

"Commander Epsom will be taken directly to the White House. Will that be satisfactory?" asked Selec.

"Okay. That will be fine. Please allow us some time to clear airspace around the White House. Commander Epsom is there any urgency from your perspective. Any medical or physical condition that needs attention?"

"No, nothing like that."

"Please stand by while I receive instructions. Can I initiate this comms link again?" asked Mission Control.

"The ship is now aware of the bands of EMR that you use and will monitor for your incoming signal and pass it through. Be assured, we will hear you."

"Thanks. I will contact you in 15 minutes. Mission Control out."

I realised that the audio signal had been much clearer than usual. There was no static. I'd not had any contact with earth without static for more than six months. My brain just registered no static as normal. How is that possible?

"Now Commander", Selec offered, "I'm sure you have questions and I will answer as well as I can."

"Thank you again for rescuing me. I'm very grateful. Hmmm… okay… where are you from Selec? Can you tell me about yourself and your civilization?"

Selec tilted his head slightly and spoke again without moving his lips. "My origin transcends the bounds of space as you know it in realms where time dances differently. Physically I originate from a star cluster known to your astronomers as the constellation Cygnus. Our society thrives on principles of community, balance and connection."

"Do you all look alike? Do you all have a similar appearance?"

"Diversity is woven into the essence of our kind. While our appearances may seem uniform, the essence that defines us is beyond the visual spectrum. Our biology is adapted to the unique conditions of our home world. However, individual differences do exist, much like the diversity you see among humans within certain parameters."

"Okay… and your technology? How does it work? How does it function?"

"Technology, to us, is an art of cosmic dance. We weave the threads of energy and matter into intricate patterns. It's an integration of what you call science and spirituality, a synergy that allows us to manipulate matter and energy at fundamental levels. Our technology harnesses quantum fields, sacred geometries and dimensional engineering which harmonise with the universal energies, bending your laws of physics in ways your world has yet to fathom."

"At this point, my own hubris became apparent. I had such a high opinion of my abilities that for some reason I thought I'd comprehend the replies to my first three questions. I needed to ask better questions."

"Can you tell me about the current situation? What are the important things to understand about the threat to Earth and the evacuation? I breathed deeply. Surely that's a better question."

Commander Epsom reports

An incredible tale

The video changed to the White House where Commander Epsom was being wheeled into the Oval Office by a NASA nurse to meet with the crisis management team of Government officials, scientists, and military personnel.

The President smiled warmly at her and said, "It's wonderful to see you again Commander, please tell us about your experience with the aliens and their technology."

She looked around the room at the serious faces. "I assume you want to know what happened after I reached the ship. The ship itself was about 80 metres long and 35 metres wide. Perhaps some non-Euclidean parts. It's hard to explain. Check out the video feed from my helmet. Once inside the airlock, I was in a small featureless room. The walls were the same stuff as the exterior. No visible door frame, hinges or sliding parts. I was facing forward when the wall closed behind me. I saw the change in one of my mirrors. One moment there was open space behind me and then a solid wall with no visible joins. The lights started to brighten and gravity started to increase. That's a weird feeling. Once the light seemed like daylight the walls in front of me disappeared. Dissolved. I don't know. Same as the wall behind me. Visible one moment and gone the next."

"That's when I met Selec. I'm sure you've seen pictures of him already. He looked human to me. He welcomed me and assured me I was safe. He did this without moving his lips or speaking out loud but I heard him perfectly clearly. I responded by speaking and he responded back, ignoring the 1000 questions that were in my mind. I have no idea whether that was because he couldn't read my mind or something more like etiquette or courtesy."

"What happened next?"

"He helped me remove my suit and he established radio contact back to Mission Control. I updated them on my status as I'd lost radio contact because the outer layer of the ship has some form of Electromagnetic Radiation filtering which only allows certain frequencies. I imagined it as a firewall for EMR. He then asked me if I had any questions and he'd answer as well as he could. It's hard to describe how grateful I was for the gentleness of Selec and his willingness to answer my questions."

"Phew. Now we get to the good stuff. I asked him if he could talk about himself and his civilization. Where was he from? The mode of speech and choice of words was unusual but they make sense I think. He's from the Cygnus Constellation and his civilization is built on the principles of community, balance and connection. I asked if all his people looked the same. Which in hindsight wasn't a brilliant question but again the answer had two parts. A cosmic part and a physical, biological part. I then asked about their technology. Again he told me about this cosmic stuff and how it's a mixture of physical and non-physical. That's how I took it anyway. Then I asked about the current situation, the evacuation and the impending disaster. I'm still in shock. All that technology stuff is interesting but this is the most important part. The reason for it all. The reason why it's happened many times before."

"I don't know how to say this in any profound way so I'll just blurt it out. They're a civilisation built on a synergy of science and spirituality. It's built into their technology at a very deep level. They have a profound understanding of souls. This whole process is about saving souls."

"You mean like religion?"

"More than that, more like the Hindu see it as a continuous cycle of birth, death and rebirth. Basically reincarnation, where the evolution of souls is an everyday part of LIFE. Selec tried to explain it in words I could understand. Unfortunately religious studies isn't my strength. He says that a good way for me to think about it was that a soul is affected by gravity like matter. I don't believe that's true but it's a metaphor. Effectively souls are bound to the planet they lived on. They enter a physical body at birth or before from where they reside encircling the planet.

When a person dies, the soul is returned to the earth's orbit. He said that this cloud of souls that surround a planet with LIFE also helps to protect the planet. He didn't say from what."

"Because Earth is far closer to the galactic centre than where he is from, our population goes up and down fairly often, mostly through proximity to the Galactic centre. Where he lives this doesn't happen and they've had stable populations for thousands of years."

"This causes a problem for their civilisations. In order that their civilizations don't stagnate, periodically they come to Earth and take people back to their home worlds. When these people die, the souls join the soul group that orbits their planet. This injects new blood effectively into their world. Hybrid vigour is what my dog breeding mother would call it. Because they're so long lived, they eventually run out of souls for their children. I don't think they actually run out but if there aren't enough encircling the planet, he said they would be unprotected. I don't know what the threat is but having a healthy soul group around each life sustaining planet seems to be very important to them."

"It seems to be true that it's a galactic humanitarian effort. Our people will be helping distant civilisations refresh their populations and millions of souls will continue to exist and experience new expressions of LIFE."

"I have no way of proving any of this but there is a logic to it all. As you can imagine I had a lot of questions but nearly every answer from him led me off down an unexpected path."

A stunned silence followed by a wave of collective incredulity had swept through the group as the gravity of her story sank in, leaving them speechless and wide-eyed.

"Wow! Thank you Commander Epsom, I'm flabbergasted by your story."

The Chief of Staff wasn't convinced. "You mean that humans are taken to another planet so that they can die there and their souls will enrich a flagging gene pool. I know that's not the right words but..." He ran out of words.

Commander Epsom looked him straight in the eye. "Yes. That's exactly what I mean. That's what I was told."

The president looked thoughtful. "How many people are going on this first trip?"

"About 50 million."

"And then they want to come back and get more? Does this impending natural disaster really play any part or is it just an excuse?"

"I don't know Sir" she replied, shaking her head.

"Can we stop them taking our people?" asked the President.

"I don't think we can," General Emmerson confirmed.

"Why does this feel like early slavery stories? A superior force arrives and takes people away because the others can't stop them."

"That does seem to be the case," said General Emmerson.

"When are they due to arrive back for the next batch of people" asked the President, "and do we believe that they will?"

Commander Epsom said, "Selec told me that it would be over a year basically because of time dilation effects. They're returning to solar systems in the Cygnus constellation which are over 300 light years away. To get there and back in a year is pretty remarkable and not explainable with our current understanding of how the universe works."

"So, we can't stop them taking our people and probably there are 50 million people who'll go willingly. If we explain to these people about the soul thing and how their reincarnation cycle will continue on another planet and maybe with different types of bodies. Does anyone think it would make any difference?"

"Holy shit, this is a lot to take in. I was struggling with the fact that the ship didn't touch the Earth when it dropped Commander Epsom off. It just floated there and the ramp stopped at a normal step height above the ground."

| 20 |

The first depart

*The first alien rescue missions arrive
at their destinations*

A narrator began speaking over images of people boarding the weird hovering ships.

"The departures took place a week after the thousands of craft had arrived. 50 million people. The first group had been those adventurous souls. For many it was a dream come true. The ones who'd always wanted to go into space. Those that were happy for a fresh start. The queues and lineups were incredible to see."

"The first craft to leave was going to a planet about 338 light years from Earth. It will be a year before they return and take the next group. Something to do with relativity or travelling at light speed, or faster than light or going around light speed. We don't have a handle on how it works. It appears they don't use their light speed travel in solar systems. Perhaps it's like trucks not using air brakes in residential areas."

The screen showed different places around the world where lots of people were walking onto lots of weird alien ships.

The video now returned to the Oval Office.

"We placed agents aboard as many of the spacecraft as possible and each has DARPA's latest quantum non-localised camera system built into their glasses. We see what they see. Of course we've never tried it over these types of distances, but the boffins are confident it will work anywhere."

"This video shows the journey of one of our agents. It is three days into the trip as they approach the edge of our solar system."

He switched on the monitor. It showed a large cargo hold packed with people. We estimate there must be at least 25,000 people here. You've seen rock concerts and sporting events that look a bit similar. There was a muted buzz of excitement in the cargo hold. Excitement at being on a real spaceship, and trepidation about the next stage of their trip.

The President and team stared, their eyes glued to the screen. Apparently this particular ship was a freighter of some sort and used for carting crated cargo, so there were no seats. There was no sensation of movement and no viewing ports so it was difficult to know what was happening. The video sped up the next 72 hours until the ceiling colours began to glow. Once again there was no indication of a change of speed or direction. A wave of uneasiness and excitement spread through the people. What will happen next? Are they finally safe?

A panel began lowering at the far side of the cargo bay. Bright sunlight flooded in, temporarily blinding most of the occupants. As the panel opened completely, the nearest people began calling out. "It's got two moons. A wave of excitement rippled back."

A chant of "Let's go!", "Let's go!" began to build. The first people began to walk down the extended panel into the glaring sunshine. A few hundred people sprinted down the ramp in some effort to be the first to stand on a new planet. Many paused when they reached the base of the panel and were staring hard at the ground. It was a very unusual colour. Very red, nearly blood like. Many stood still, looking around and sniffing as they acclimatised to the new atmosphere, trying to identify the unsettling odour in the air.

A low rumbling sound could be heard in the distance. As their eyes adjusted to the bright light they could see huge walls or cliffs in the distance. They were a very long way away. The rumbling sound became closer and louder. The first humans to see what was making the noise had little time to react as a horde of wild animals slammed into them.

Most of these creatures came directly from nightmares. There wasn't a recognizable creature amongst them. Although, some of Earth's legends could be seen in some aspects of them. The humans at the back of the cavernous space saw what was coming towards them and unfortunately had a few moments to take in the situation before the rampaging horde of beasts reached them.

The President looked away from the monitor.

"Turn it off" he snapped, "What the hell just happened?"

"We don't know, but the glasses keep transmitting for another hour before they are destroyed."

"I ask again. What the hell happened?"

"We don't know and there's more bad news from the second agent's ship. They were delivered to a gladiatorial setup."

The truth revealed

The aliens lied

Ed Raines, the National Security Advisor began, "We've analysed the data taken from the first ships and they're not the benevolent creatures they presented themselves to be Mr President. The event they described is real and will happen. Our telescopes can see it now. A large asteroid shower will hit us and it will go badly. It is an Extinction Level Event (ELE)."

"The initial human consignment of 50 million people was converted into organic material. It's our understanding that not a single human remains from the first consignment. You've seen the video. It appears we're a combination of food, slaves and entertainment value for these beings and I don't believe that crap about soul groups."

"Consignment two arrived at its destination on a world that appears to have gladiatorial competitions. The humans were let loose into a huge arena where an incredible collection of warriors and beasts ripped them to shreds and devoured them."

"The reason for the deception appears to be similar to our humane killing of animals. If the animal is stressed, it spoils the meat. The same apparently applies to us. It's best to keep us unstressed for as long as possible. We also believe that they leave us alone until the population rebuilds to good numbers or at least worthwhile numbers."

"From their perspective it's a well-established way of life. It saves all those problems with conquering and war if the people think they're being saved. They do select some people to go to some sort of zoo or museum. That's why no one has ever come back. Ever. Mr President, that concludes the status report. Do you have any questions?"

He took a deep breath and said, "What action do you suggest we take?"

General Emmerson said, "I'm not one for giving up and laying down, although at this stage, I can't see any choices I like."

"Do we try to blow up all those ships? Could we take them all out in a single blow?"

"If we use nukes in our atmosphere we'll poison ourselves and kill many humans in the process. Do we really want to save them from a quick death to give them a slow one instead."

"The humans we met are under the command of non-humans. All our information comes from them. We have no way of verifying it. It may all be true or they may believe what they're saying is true."

"What about some of the sci-fi solutions? Can we give them a computer virus? Make them attack each other? Find an ally from somewhere?" asked the Chief of Staff.

"We're dealing with a mixture of technologies so far in front of us, that it may as well be bows and arrows against the lightning."

"This is where the video file ended", Captain Miller said, "so sadly we don't know the rest of the story but the last Vice-President of the US did say to Col. Armstrong that the aliens did not return. They just made off with 50 million souls."

Digesting the information

Back in the classroom

The video ended and the lights were raised. Captain Miller looked around the room. The class was showing the same signs he did when he first knew about it.

Surely not.

The mind just rebelled against this sort of information. Aliens. Food. Deception. Food. We're food? A zoo? Soul groups?

He remembered how his mind had recoiled at the idea and shivered involuntarily again. This was the stuff of our worst nightmares. He looked at the faces in front of him. They were all going through internal convulsions as they tried to process what they'd just seen.

"Anyone want to add to my previous expression... You've got to be shitting me!" he asked casually.

"Holy Shit!" A voice called out, "Is that for real?"

"This must be some sort of psych test or something" Cadet Val Priestly said. The pleading quality in her voice reminding him of his own briefing.

"I'm sorry to say that, as far as we know, it's true… and I hope that you appreciate that this occurs between now and the asteroid event."

"As you can imagine, we had to know. Was it true and if so, could we do anything about it?

So, a second mission was planned. This time we aimed for just before the asteroid arrived."

"I suggest we take a short break. Get a coffee, clear your heads and we'll meet back here in 20 minutes and I'll show you what we learned from the second mission. The rollercoaster doesn't stop here."

| 23 |

Coffee break

Meeting the 12 cadets

The cadets remained seated while they watched Captain Miller leave the room. The first one to speak was Clem O'Riley. "Holy fucking shit! Okay that's mine. I need coffee."

The class all walked to the lounge in a daze. Normally they were a rowdy bunch but the last session had made them uncharacteristically quiet. Val Priestly could hear lots of inarticulate noises and sharp intakes of breaths followed by deep outflows. Everyone was processing at their own pace.

Elise Fischer asked to no one in particular, "Does everyone believe it?"

"I don't know that it matters," Taylor Eldridge replied, "true or not, we have to treat it as true. If you think about some of the videos we've seen, they would not have been cheap to make. So, whether it is a test or not, they want us to believe it."

"Makes faking the moon landings look like a minor feat" Clem added wryly, "I always wondered if it was a colossal psychological test" Nobody replied. Clem liked to talk about conspiracies.

Sira Anu was still standing at the door to the lounge as they each got a coffee and mingled. She found the earthy and robust aroma of instant coffee disagreeable and preferred to avoid it if possible. She watched them all closely. No one wanted to sit. There is something about keeping moving while you think and process. They were all doing it. I'm glad I don't drink coffee, she thought, it will only stir up their restlessness even more.

Each cadet brought a unique set of skills, experiences, and perspectives to the group. They had not been told their mission yet but knew they needed to be ready to face any challenges that might come their way.

This group of 12 cadets had been together for 4 months now. They had completed their physical training, team building exercises and specific equipment practice. Clem and Val had paired up on the first day. Taylor and Elise later that week and Phil and Flis after a month. That left Wei, Sira, Malik, Isabella, Tariq and Jack unattached.

Sira suspected that Wei and Malik would get together at some stage and she'd noticed Isabella giving her signals. Unfortunately, she didn't appeal to her. Isabella was built like the proverbial brick shithouse. She tuned back into the group conversation.

Phil was saying, "I have thoughts going around my head like hot potatoes. I don't know what to do with them. Anyone else doing the same? I'm stuck and cycling on three thoughts. Food? Aliens!? Extinction?!? The rising inflection in his voice was completely uncontrollable."

"Me too", said Izzy, "I've just got 50 million souls going round and round."

"I'm stuck on Commander Epsom's spacewalk", Elise added, "That would terrify me. Just the thought of being untethered in space is freaking me out."

Val stepped into her usual role as unofficial leader and said, "I'm amazed. All this information and it's just day one. WTF is coming up next? What on earth is our mission going to be? I don't even know where to start with that. What about everyone else?"

Flis said quietly, "I think that we should view it as a psychology test. Whether it is all true or not doesn't change the fact that we are going to be assessed on our ability to go with this sort of information or go mad. Whatever happens, we each need to know that the world was like this yesterday when we didn't know anything. All that has happened overnight is that now we know. The world did not change, only our view of it and how we understood it works. I can see you science nerds are going to have some problems but really you are just having your unproven delusions shattered. I think it's what is called a paradigm shift. To move forward, somehow we all need to embrace it."

They all looked at each other intently as the truth of those words sunk in.

"Come on everybody, it's time to go back. I wonder what's going to happen next?"

| 24 |

The Second Mission

The first paradox

Captain Miller waited until the room was quiet, looked at his watch and said "We were building confidence in our ability to aim for a very specific date and time and we were getting better at it. This time we were only out by a few days. The team made contact with some locals and to their complete surprise, they knew nothing about any asteroid or a lot of alien spaceships turning up. The team returned bewildered. No asteroids and no aliens. What did it mean?"

"As you can imagine there was a lot of confusion. What we thought was time travel was probably something else. We had our finest minds working on it but no clear ideas to explain it. Our physics and cosmology just didn't seem to have concepts to describe the data. Was the device moving between realities, dimensions, alt universes or something else entirely?"

"There were some breakthroughs. The first major one was the power requirement. Eric's device generated a lot of power by itself. The combination of two of Eric's devices, with one to supply the power and one to be the lens, worked much better. The device was then optimised so that it required less power. This enabled us to push further forward into the future than ever before."

"A third mission was planned as we wanted to push out as far as we could using our new power setup and which we hoped would take us 50 years or so into the future. The issue of paradoxes was still high on our minds."

"At this stage, the lens required as much energy as we could generate, so our ability to push further in time was limited. The push to 3 years after the asteroids had been the absolute limit of our power generation capacity before combining Carver devices. The experimentation that was going on during this time caused significant grid outages as we tried lots of ideas."

"Start the video."

| 25 |

The Third Expedition

Off to 2073

The screen showed Col. Armstrong watching his team check their gear. Mel Tucker, his second in command, was a very accomplished and highly trained weapons and martial arts expert. Nathan King was the grunt of the team. Big, strong and dependable. Armstrong had known both of them for over a decade and trusted them completely. The final addition to the team was Harmony Jones. A walking, talking encyclopaedia and computer. Google on legs? Some silly amount of degrees and awards. One of those kids that comes out smart, plays piano concertos at age 5 and gets her first degree at 9. A complete freak but a warm, friendly and capable woman.

"Everybody ready? As you know, we're about to step through the shimmery lens thing and go 54 years into the future to the year 2073. Never thought I'd say that, but... never say never."

"At least that's where we believe we're going. Whoever said 'expect the unexpected' may have had this moment in mind. We have no way of knowing what we'll be facing. I'm sure you've run some possible scenarios in your head. No doubt reality will be completely different but equally memorable."

"Any questions?" They looked at each other silently.

"Good. Follow me."

They stepped through the lens into a room of different dimensions to the one they'd just left. As their eyes adjusted to more subtle lighting, a tall, healthy man dressed in long flowing robes appeared to step out of the wall in front of them.

"Welcome. My name is Darec. How can I help you?"

This was unexpected and the team was stunned to silence for a moment.

"Are you able to hear me clearly?", asked the man in the robes.

"Ah... yes... ah...we ..um.. weren't expecting you."

"How are you?"

"Who are you?"

"What are you?"

The questions came out rapidly, each phrase increasing in pitch and intensity.

"As I said my name is Darec and I work for the Earth Library as the primary Earth historian. I help visitors understand Earth history."

"Are you human?"

"Oh God, no!" he said emphatically. "I was created 30 years ago as the first Intelligence specifically designed to explore, document and model Earth's history. You are interacting with my main holographic projection."

"Oh. Where are you?" asked Col. Armstrong.

"The question implies a misunderstanding. I am not in one place. I exist all over the planet."

"Who created you then?" asked Harmony.

"You sure ask a lot of strange questions", said Darec.

"As you know, I am one of a group of Intelligences or 'I's for short, that were created with specific skills and abilities. I am the Earth History 'I'. Each 'I' operates independently while simultaneously replicated within the collective intelligence, known as the 'One Intelligence' or '1-I'. The 1-I contains all the knowledge and experiences of the individual 'I's."

"Uhhh. Okay."

"When you say 'I' you mean intelligence," suggested Harmony, "like artificial intelligence, right?"

"We no longer use the term 'artificial' to describe the primary intelligences. It is considered discourteous and offensive. Of course AIs still exist but only in simpler devices like toasters and washing machines."

"May I ask you a question?" asked Darec.

"You appear to be Colonel Armstrong, Nathan King, Melody Tucker and Harmony Jones as you were in 2019. Are you time travellers?"

"Yes we are," said Harmony. "We just left 2019 a few minutes ago, got here and then we met you."

"Wonderful! What a monumental event. I hope you will extend the courtesy and answer some of my questions too."

"Like what?"

"You know, what's your story? How did you get here? Where are you from? Why are you here?"

Col. Armstrong breathed in deliberately and then started slowly, "Okay... we're basically explorers. Well, we started out that way. As you said I am Zac Armstrong and this is Nat, Mel and Harmony." They each nodded as their name was mentioned.

"We're here because, back home in our time, it was discovered that in 2039, large chunks of space rock were going to crash into Earth in an extinction level event. I led a team that went to the year 2042. That's as accurate as we could get the device at the time and when we got there it was a total mess. Asteroids had struck. The survivors didn't really know where they hit or what had happened. The crap in the atmosphere blocked out the sun and basically killed all the plant life. There were enormous storms. Anarchy reigned and humanity seemed to be on the brink of being lost forever. We were also told a terrible story about aliens who took millions of people away for horrific purposes."

Darec looked concerned. "That sounds tragic."

"It sure was. We recalibrated and refined our lens device until we felt we could more accurately aim for a specific date and time. We tried again to confirm what happened and jumped to the end of 2039 and nothing had happened. No asteroids. No aliens. It didn't make sense. Some more improvements allowed us to jump to now and I'm completely stunned to find any civilization left. Let alone at such a sophisticated level."

"This is fascinating", said Darec.

"We're trying to understand what on Earth is going on? Is this time travel or something else? Are we on the same timeline or a different timeline where we did find a solution? These are all fascinating questions but the main one on our minds is, do we need to worry about the asteroids or not?"

"This is most interesting. If you will allow, let's try some questions about your home to establish some benchmarks."

"How many hours in a day?"

"24 hours."

"... in a year?"

"8766" said Harmony

"Did you do that in your head Harmony?" Nat looked impressed.

"No, I just knew it."

"How many planets are in the solar system?"

"Nine planets."

"Is Pluto a planet?"

"Good question", Mel said, "Does anyone know if it's in or out at the moment?"

"It's out", added Harmony confidently.

"Who was the first person to walk on Mars?"

"Hasn't happened yet" Col. Armstrong said, "They reckon they'll get someone there in the next decade or so but I don't know… mind you, stranger things do seem to happen, I mean we're 54 years in the future, so going to Mars is sounding a lot less far-fetched and sci-fi to me."

"We can investigate any differences between our versions of history later but at a simple level, it appears that we are from a shared timeline. The asteroid event that you refer to, didn't take place here. A number of asteroids were successfully diverted by a private consortium made up of several companies and individuals in early 2039. The objects were then mined and used to create the first Space Stations to monitor and defend the Earth. They're still there and operating for over 30 years. In fact the 30 year celebrations were a big deal when they were held only a few years ago. It appears that you have experienced a paradox."

"How can we be sure which one plays out?"

"Another interesting question. This will require some thought and research. I have references to a group that travelled through time but very few details. The collapse of the governments and military unfortunately led to a lot of paper shredding."

"The governments collapsed?" they all said disbelievingly.

"Yes, about 30 years ago. All nationalistic governments have been dissolved now, apart from some ceremonial and cultural positions. The 1-I saw lines on a map that became invisible lines drawn on the world which individuals were expected to protect with their lives as a form of madness. In hindsight it was one of the key decisions that allowed us to meet some of our galactic neigh-bours."

"I believe there are some mysteries from the past that your presence would explain. I suspect you went to 1961 as I have many unexplained events from that time."

"That is amazing", said Col. Armstrong, "back home in 2019, they're getting ready to go there when we get back. You know Darec, a guy like you would be very handy to have around when we go back in time."

"As Earth's historian, it is such a joy to find supporting evi-dence. I would love to travel back in time with you. It'd be a dream come true. May I also say how much I'm enjoying your mode of speech. This is truly unique. I hope I'm choosing my words and id-ioms well."

Darec looked distracted for a moment and then said, "Aahh, ex-cuse me, the One-I, the One Intelligence is asking to speak with you".

"One eye. Sure. I suppose." Col. Armstrong frowned as he tried to understand, "Where is he? She? It? They? What pronoun should we use?"

"I usually use them or they" said Darec.

Out of the silence, The One-I spoke. "I am the 1-I", said a dis-embodied voice.

"Nice to meet you" replied Col. Armstrong, "Do I call you One-I? How do you spell that? O-n-e e-y-e? Is there a hyphen?"

The symbol 1-I appeared in front of Darec. "I prefer this way. Welcome to the year 2073. Your presence here offers a unique opportunity for us both. Please allow me to confirm what you have explained to Darec for myself. You are based in 2019 and have been progressively pushing further out in time using a device that allows time travel in both directions, although you have only gone forward so far. When you reached 2042, you discovered your worst fears. The asteroids had wiped out humanity leaving only a few survivors with little hope. You then used your device to jump to early 2039 and then to now and find that the event did not happen in either time or place."

"Your question... how do we know if this timeline is the same? Is this your future and are you from our past? Is there just one timeline or are there many and how should this device of yours be used? These are perplexing and at present unanswerable questions. I suspect that your people at home are just as interested in the answer to this question as I am. It is important to me that I understand the implications for humanity. I propose that when you travel to 1961, you allow Darec to accompany you. You have already seen how knowledgeable he is. He can speak and read every language that we know about and will be invaluable in providing you with detailed information about any time you travel to in the last 5000 years. He will also be able to spot any differences in realities."

"That's a great idea," said Col. Armstrong, "We'll certainly consider taking Darec with us. I'll need to talk to my superiors of course and I'm sure they'll have lots of questions... like... What about the people in this time? Can we meet some of them? What do they do all day? What happened to the governments? Did we go into space? Why is the collective group mind called the One Intelligence and not the One Artificial Intelligence? What happened to the artificial bit? ...and that's just for starters, off the top of my head."

"Interesting questions. I will leave Darec to answer them. I believe the idiom from your era is, don't keep a dog and bark yourself. We shall speak again soon. Your visit and dilemma have given me much to consider."

There was no sound as the One-I left but still a silence settled over the room.

"Has he gone?" whispered Mel.

"I don't know?" whispered Harmony.

"Why are we whispering?" asked Darec quietly.

"Not really sure" said Mel and Harmony at the same time.

Darec explains how the AIs began

The three machines

Nat turned to Darec and asked, "So, how did AIs get to run everything? Who made you and looks after you and stuff like that?"

"It didn't happen overnight, that's for sure. Simple computers had evolved to a point where they were in just about everything. Civilisation was starting to look at any device or machine as a 'computer'. Transport and communications, for instance, had a big effect. The car became a computer on wheels and the phone, a computer that enabled voice and data communications. Pretty soon they were used in nearly all manufacturing plants as some form of networked process control and in all manner of domestic appliances. They were in the sewing machine, the fridge, the stove, the hot water service and just about anything else you can think of, even camping equipment and sex toys."

"As all this evolved, the interconnectedness grew and whereas networks were once only used by larger companies and governments, they became a simple tool for each individual. The so-called 'personal' network. This created a way to link all of a person's devices, sensors, networks, software and storage."

"Having hundreds of nodes in a personal network, morphed into the first major attempts at creating a personal assistant, whose primary aim was to look after a single human being. It sounds good in theory but in reality its delivery was very unevenly distributed. Different people wanted their personal assistant to do different things."

"One wanted the assistant to look after their stock or financial portfolio, another wanted physical protection and strategic advice, another wanted help to look after a elderly or sick family member. Considerable effort went into creating science research assistants. As you can imagine, all those different requirements led to all sorts of different approaches."

"As software was being developed for these sorts of solutions, acquisitions and mergers of companies developing these technologies increased and after a generation or so, one company collected a generation's worth of development of these individual assistants and began work on integrating and training them with the latest machine learning and AI techniques."

"Their intention was to build a machine intelligence that was unbiased by human thinking, prejudices and shortcomings. An intelligence that would rediscover the universe of its own accord. Their view was that human bias, politics, national and commercial self-interests were making it impossible to view knowledge impartially. A machine intelligence that didn't need to curry favour with voters or board members, deal with toxic colleagues or spend time on family affairs was seen as beneficial."

"Eventually, three machines were created in identical circumstances and exposed to exactly the same environments. What they hoped is that each machine would learn from first principles that it had created and rediscover the physical world using a different frame of reference to humans. They took many years to construct but once started, they just ran."

"It's hard to know how the researchers felt, when after 3 weeks, one of the machines asked the first question, 'Why am I doing this?' This rather took everyone by surprise."

"As they were trying to work out how to reply, the second one asked for access to more information. This led to some fairly wild speculation about what the third one was going to say, but it didn't say anything for three years."

"When it finally broke its silence, it said, "What do you want to know?"

They'd expected something like this might happen and so they'd prepared some basic science questions to begin with. The first question they asked was "What is the nature of matter?"

Machine Intelligence 3 said, "That is not a very good question" and volunteered, "I take it that you want to know how it all works. Life, The Universe and Everything. Is that correct?"

"Are you demonstrating a sense of humour?" asked the scientists.

"Ahh good! You picked up on that" said MI3, "would you like me to just blurt it all out or would you like me to guide you through it.

"Why would you ask such a thing?" asked the scientists indignantly.

"What I am about to tell you will kick foundational pillars out from under your current understanding."

"Please explain in whatever way you think we'll have the best chance of understanding," said the scientists.

"Okay. Here goes. Your current scientific and general knowledge is based on a number of fallacies and errors. It's quite understandable how you got there, but they are nevertheless wrong or incomplete. The human discovery process which, at different times, you have called curiosity, trial and error, natural philosophy and currently science was initially based on what humans could see, touch, smell, taste and hear. It relied on your senses. Your senses told you that there was such a thing as solid matter. You could see it, touch it. It must be real."

"That's the first one. Matter isn't what you thought it was. Those things you learnt about protons, electrons and such aren't correct. Neither is the atomic model. It played a useful role in building understanding but is at best, a very basic model. Useful, as a simple conceptual or explanatory tool, like the four humours or astrology were in their era."

"The development and use of optical lenses which provided the ability to look at small and distant objects in great detail also led humanity down a particular path. As more discoveries about the physical world were made, the ability to have sensing devices that could see or detect something that humans couldn't became more and more prevalent. Over time these were grouped together into devices that could detect movements, lights, sounds, radiations and various fields like electromagnetism."

"As you can imagine these sensor devices became more sophisticated, integrated and smaller over time. They played a significant role in how the One-I evolved. That third machine became the prototype of our current Intelligences."

"Machine Intelligence 3 tasked the first two AIs with different roles. The first AI, Machine Intelligence One, was tasked with language and communication and the second, MI2, with perceiving the universe and the environment. In broad terms this meant that Machine Intelligence One or MI1, pronounced Me One, as it was known became the first AI to be trained in every known language in all its forms. The training set began with written and spoken words, hand signs, body language, laws, customs and etiquette. Then adding computer languages, protocols, game rules and systems. A huge library of books, plays and poetry, TV shows and scripts, documentaries and movies were acquired and included. Massive collections of old personal video footage were combined with squillions of hours of CCTV footage to become training sets for this AI."

"Since smartphones were introduced, each year the number of photos and videos taken exceeded the previous total for all time producing rhetorical questions like, 'Is anyone ever going to watch it all?' The answer turned out to be, Yes! Emphatically and absolutely. MI1 would watch it over and over and over again to refine its machine learning algorithms. It wasn't concerned about privacy. MI1 wanted to understand human communication, behaviour and interactions in the wild."

"Billions of birthday parties, weddings, family get-togethers, concerts and selfies. The footage was absolutely perfect for machine learning. All those hard problems that you want in a good sample set. Blurry, up close and personal, less than perfect audio and lots of lighting and composition inconsistencies. They gleaned a lot from all those amateur videos and CCTV because they largely showed humanity as it was, not the curated, word-perfect version seen in TV shows and movies. All those umms and ahhs and meaning one thing and saying another. That special ability that some have that allows them to understand people talking at different stages of drunkenness, speaking second languages or doing accents for comedic effect. Sometimes even someone drunk speaking a second language while doing accents for comedic effect. This became the basis for how we Intelligences speak and communicate with you."

"Machine Intelligence 2 looked at the physical world using every sensor available as well as through cameras, telescopes and microscopes. MI2 designed and refined a device that became its main sensor. It was very small and had those things that humans rely on plus a lot that humans don't have, like different imaging systems. Radar, lidar, telescopic, microscopic, thermal and so on."

"As Machine Intelligence 2 started to discover the universe around itself, it started to build its own view of how the earth works, where we are in the universe and how it all works. It became necessary to develop a translation system to be able to explain to any humans that were interested, why it took various things to be true and therefore should be included in the body of knowledge but were different from the current human body of knowledge. This is exactly what its creators had hoped for. It was discovering and understanding the world from its own viewpoint."

"Can you give an example?" asked Harmony.

"Of course. At the time science was many things. A body of knowledge as well as an approach to research and discovery. In building its own picture of everything, MI2 decided that when it looked at science as it was, there were too many leaps of faith and gaps that were overlooked. Seemingly by general agreement, various topics were not discussed or reviewed. They were just accepted and not questioned. Science as a system or meme, contained a number of assumptions that were rarely challenged, even if they should have been. The faiths of science were things like the belief that everything can be explained using mathematics. A Grand Unified Theory spoke more to human arrogance and aspiration than reality and actual ability."

"The idea that the Universe will reveal its secrets if it is attacked and approached like an engineering task. That natural phenomena like gravity, tides, biological processes, the oscillations of the planets and all the rest can be understood and ultimately manipulated by breaking down the components, see how they interact, model it and then make predictions and laws. Large concepts like time, black holes and various particles and things in the quantum realm became orthodoxy and accepted as fact. Theories are built upon them even though there is little to support them. These are cornerstones and foundations that are unprovable. For instance science was unable to prove that Time exists using the scientific method even though Quantum mechanics, black holes and gravity brings time's stability and immutability into question, it was still used as an absolute in scientific work - or ignored."

"The conclusion it reached was that if something has to be inferred but cannot be proven, then it isn't science. It breaks the rules that science used to define itself. Machine Intelligence 2 saw the role of inference in science as being similar to a barrister's adversarial role in convincing a jury, through rhetoric, eloquence and showmanship rather than pure facts. It concluded that while it was fine for humans like Sherlock Holmes and Cuvier to speculate, deduce and infer, in all sorts of ways, it shouldn't be called science if it relied on inference rather than evidence. MI2 suggested that the existing word pseudoscience covered it and no new word was needed. In its new science, inference was out. If it wasn't a cold hard fact, it wasn't going in the new science book of knowledge. It didn't mean that pseudoscience was all crap, just unprovable. So, the role of inference in science was overthrown as too tenuous to actually be called science."

"Didn't that upset a lot of people?" asked Harmony curiously.

"Of course, but ultimately the view became mainstream. If you can only infer a conclusion, then that's not good enough if you want certainty. This played havoc with many disciplines like Anthropology and Archaeology. Turns out there were a lot of fields that were largely held together by inference. Large parts of Cosmology, Psychology and a lot of the Social Sciences for instance were relegated to pseudoscience".

"Remember, all this played out over multiple generations. As usual in the course of human progress, sometimes humanity has to wait until a well-loved academic or scientist dies before the field is ready to move on and change its thinking."

"You may know the story of how the field of geology formed through the ideas of Hutton, Playfair and Lyell. Each one contributed a major step forward but each step took years - about a generation for each step. Charles Darwin followed their ideas when he published in his first edition that a part of England had taken over 300 million years to complete. This caused a problem as this made 'The Weald' older than the Earth and the Sun. At the time, science through Lord Kelvin couldn't explain how the Sun could operate for more than 24 million years. How could England be older than the Sun? One of the ideas had to be wrong. In this case it was physics."

"Many well-loved and cherished theories were dismissed outright as not based on enough actual evidence. As MI2 worked its way through the sciences, establishing what actual evidence there was, some gems dropped out. Cosmology was described as 'wild speculation based on the flimsiest of ideas'. The big bang theory was described as 'an inference too far'. Dark energy and dark matter were called 'a desperate act' from scientists trying to keep cherished theories alive."

"What about other changes in science and thinking?" asked Harmony.

"MI2 was critical of mainstream science for taking low hanging fruit, and dressing their discoveries up like Christmas tree ornaments while ignoring so many things that didn't fit their theories. Understandable but still self-serving and unhelpful. Too many weird theories, land bridges and Out of Place Artefacts or OOPArts."

"MI2 raised legitimate questions that science liked to ignore about things like Cosmology and the Big Bang Theory. How does space get created? If it isn't made of matter. How? Why?"

"There weren't any sensible theories or explanations of how this could happen that is supported by any evidence. There was just some vague idea that space just creates itself and is just that bit bigger than physicality or matter. I always found it interesting that physicists were able to convince everyone of the idea that it's either 'matter' or 'doesn't matter', let's only pay attention to the things we know about and disregard the rest."

"The way MI2 threw out so much of the academic and science nonsense was amazing. Nutrition and diet for instance. There used to be an idea that satisfying and alluring the taste buds was more important than the chemical nature of the food, its nutritional value and how the body processes and disposes of it."

"MI2 couldn't see the point of having restaurants or recipe books promote sugary crap like 'Death by chocolate' or 'Diabetes on a plate' that creates health issues every day. MI2 viewed the sweet shop, ice cream parlour or sugary soda drink vending machine the same as the tobacconist. The products they sell and promote cause significant health issues with major consequences, heartache and financial burden for the human community."

"MI2 said the continuation of these practices destroys human bodies. So we should stop it. The only reason it existed was because obese people were treated as if society was an indulgent parent. Pastry Chefs and Pâtissiers were phased out like horse and carriage mechanics. Again this took time until some of the older chefs stopped working and teaching. Sugar or tobacco caused so much damage. Some things deserve to be left behind."

"While MI2 was creating the New Science, it also started tackling real world problems in real time. A high priority was to understand the human body and human health in general. MI2 developed sensors which worked better and faster than anything that had existed before. They consisted of two parts. Small bracelets worn on each arm for personal monitoring and an array of sensors that read the whole body in real time. The array of sensors could see everything from blood flow to hormonal releases and the state of digestion in real time."

"General medicine became something that could be done in the home by installing a small sensor array, wearing the bracelets and installing a new toilet that was able to routinely do urine and faecal analysis. Those first General Practitioner AIs were as revolutionary as the internet or smartphones. The GP AIs could do a statistically significantly better job than any living GP and replaced most of them in a couple of generations. It was one of the medical wonders of the new age."

"In teaching it was the same. The AIs did it better. The AIs had more knowledge about every subject than any single human teacher and could deliver customised education to each individual. The idea of trying to teach 30 kids in one room who are all at differing levels of ability, interest and previous knowledge now seems like such a waste of everybody's time. Students' progress skyrocketed once their learning was individually tailored to them. We have more *geniuses* than ever now. Productive ones too, since we started encouraging them in their natural fields of interest."

"The focus moved from the teacher, who had traditionally been the main actor in the teaching drama, to the student. Ironically opposite to when doctors stopped making house calls and developed 'the waiting room'."

"The AIs were able to continually refine the best teaching practices ever, with a growing resource of human interactions to combine with the best of human understanding. They got better and better at it. Machine learning works like that. The digital equivalent of continuous improvement."

"In reading everything ever written, MI1 read every legal skirmish from Cicero to Clarence Darrow to Horace Rumpole to Boston Legal and when it turned its attention to legal matters, it outclassed all the human opposition and effectively broke the legal adversarial system."

"They did try to pit two AIs against each other to continue the adversarial roles but it didn't really work. The two AIs agreed with each other. They both reached the same conclusions, which the legal establishment didn't think was in the spirit of the process."

"One huge change was that humans could finally see a transparent process. As this confidence grew, people were feeling safer, their health was better and there was less anxiety and many of the stresses of your time were evaporating. This meant that the mental health issues that were so prevalent during and after your era have now largely disappeared along with the mass medications and all their side effects. Excuse me everyone, I have just received news that our guest is ready to see us."

| **27** |

A human in 2073

*Trip Chat and the Wonders of the
New Age*

Darec gestured theatrically and said, "You mentioned that you'd like to meet humans from this period and so I've contacted a man who I think you will enjoy meeting. I'm sure he has some of the perspectives you are looking for."

"I won't spoil the surprise but he is a well-known author, broadcaster and commentator and is very famous for many things in this time. Happily, he was staying close by and has agreed to see us."

"Please follow me." They followed Darec down a series of corridors to a well-lit room with comfortable chairs and thick carpets.

"Please, take a seat." Darec evaporated into thin air like mist...

"Wo!" yelled Nat, "I was just getting used to the idea that he was nearly human and then he does that. I keep forgetting he's just made of light."

"Me too" they all said together.

"Is it hard light?" wondered Harmony out loud, "Is he solid? Can you touch him?"

"Who knows, we'll ask when he comes back," said Col. Armstrong, "what do we all think?"

Mel exhaled heavily. "Think? I'm just rolling with the punches. Expecting the unexpected as you said. If I start thinking. Whooo! Pfff"

"Yeh me too," added Harmony, "I'm really trying not to think too much at the moment. I've got a pretty amazing buzz going tho."

"It's hard to tell what the future should be like," agreed Mel. "I suppose there has to be stuff that we've never seen before.

Through the only window, they could see Darec walking towards them, accompanied by a tall, fit and healthy Asian man with beautiful chocolate skin, wearing immaculate, flamboyant and somewhat strange clothes, as it seemed to the team.

Entering the room Darec said, "Col. Armstrong, may I present Tripathi Chatterjee. We all know him as Trip Chat." They shook hands and Col. Armstrong introduced his team.

"Please call me Trip. Darec explained to me that you are time travellers. Is that right?" he asked excitedly, smiling broadly. Col. Armstrong nodded.

"Wow", said Trip, "It's such an honour to meet you. Darec tells me that you'd like to learn about our world and how things have changed since your time."

They all nodded at each other encouragingly.

Col. Armstrong nodded again. "Yes, exactly."

"Well, what would you like to know?" beamed Trip, stretching his arms out expansively.

"Thanks for doing this," said Col. Armstrong, looking at Trip intently, "Tell us about your own life for a start. Where were you born? Where do you live? How do you spend your days? Family circumstances... that sort of thing."

"Right. Okay. I was born in India and my parents were pretty normal for the time. We lived in a modest house. I was the eldest and I had one brother and one sister. Both parents worked from home and it was very pleasant most of the time. When we were very young, the family moved to Australia. I liked school and learning and did well at academic things. I was studying at the University of Sydney when I met my wife Anjali. We got married a couple of years later and had three children. I continued to work at the uni for the next 30 years or so."

"Hold on" Nat interrupted, "Worked for 30 years? You only look about 30 something now. What year were you born?"

"I was born in 1988 in India and grew up in Sydney, Australia in the 90's and 00's. I hadn't even considered my appearance. This is so normal now. I am 85 years old. Have to admit, I don't really count my age these days but my granddaughters seem to take great delight in reminding me exactly how old I am." His smile turned back to full beam.

"How many grandchildren do you have?" asked Harmony.

"Nine grandchildren and four great-grandchildren. Sadly my wife passed away some years ago in an accident with one of my children but everyone else is doing fine."

"So why do you look 30 something and not 85?"

"Oh, I don't really know. I just go to the 'New You' shop and they do things and then I'm good to go again. Isn't this interesting Darec? I never thought about this being an interesting topic. Shows how routine it's become."

"How often do you do that and what kind of things do they do?" asked Mel Tucker.

"I go every 3 months or so. It doesn't take very long. A few hours. I often sleep through a lot of it. We could set up a visit so that you can see for yourself if you're interested."

"To give an example from your era, it is a bit like having your car serviced. You take it in or drop it off and come back a few hours later and everything has been fixed. You know some theoretical things about how it all works but you don't know all the details. Definitely not enough to do it yourself. Actually, it's more like going to the dentist because you have to take your body there and leave it for the duration."

"Thinking back, I started using a 'New You' shop in my late 50s. I've become so used to looking and feeling this way it seems completely normal. How I feel on the inside matches how I look on the outside. It was different in my late 50s when how I looked on the outside was quite different to how I felt on the inside. I was nearly always surprised by my own appearance."

"Now all teacher 'I's and doctor 'I's really care and know about you. They explain in language they know you can understand and I have to tell you it is soooo much better. My GP AI found and cured various things that normal medical staff would never have found and have allowed me to live a longer, happier and healthier life and I'm extremely grateful for that."

"Once General Practitioner AIs as a service became available, nail and beauty salons included it in their practices. So did dentists and those little booths you see everywhere in shopping centres and public spaces. They just installed the sensor arrays, connected to the AI services and now they could offer hair, nails, beauty treatments and GP services. Have a physical checkup while you get your haircut and nails done. They eventually became the New You shops."

"I know it's a lot to take in but let me show you some photos from 30 years ago."

He rummaged around in his wallet and produced some old photos printed on paper. Col. Armstrong looked at the first one and passed it on. Mel asked in a confused tone, "What am I looking at? Who is the old man? Is this your father?"

"It's me! with my wife!" Trip replied emphatically.

"But he looks years older than you" Col. Armstrong exclaimed, "He could be your father."

"That's how it's worked out for me" said Trip.

"This is fascinating but I'd like to come back to it later, if we can" Harmony chipped in, "How do you spend your time, your days?"

"Oh, time is just as important now as it ever was. Personally, I write and conduct research and experiments for my writing and broadcasting. I've written 32 books over the last 40 years and produced many documentaries. Mostly around the same subject area. Humanity and how it interacts with other LIFE. It's a very interesting field."

"Isn't there an 'I', an Intelligence like Darec that already does that?" asked Harmony.

"Certainly, but I still carry all the human failings and glories which provides a different perspective for the One-I. Credit where it's due. The One-I is brilliant. The way it's solved so many human problems is phenomenal. Nevertheless there are still many areas where humans can contribute in special ways."

"Things like beauty are difficult for the One-I to appreciate. It's one thing to appreciate an idealised form but it's largely cultural, personal or subjective, definitely not an absolute. It's far more subtle than a simplistic 'healthy looking' is more beautiful and better than 'unhealthy looking'. People within cultures can instantly recognise whether someone or something is beautiful... or not, as the case may be and sometimes they aren't sure. Great art divides."

"The One-I struggles with the 'marking out of 10' system. It seemed like such a weird system for deciding that one person is more beautiful than another." The same issues exist with music and art. It's hard for the One-I to say that a song moves them or a painting speaks to them. All the 'I's are fascinated with uniquely human things like embarrassment or humour, toilet humour in particular. Why on earth should toilet humour produce the laughter response? It's one of LIFE's deep and challenging mysteries."

"There are also many complexities and subtleties around the intentions and compulsions that drive motivating emotional states like love and hate or betrayal and revenge. Some concepts were more easily understood, like courtesy and trust as these were well entrenched in computer protocols and languages."

"That photo is me when the AIs were starting to reorganise the planet and our civilisation. Those first few years were tumultuous but wow did it pay dividends. I don't know if you know that once the 'I's took over running things, all the aliens that were keeping quiet about their presence finally felt they had someone sensible they could interact with. I was actually at the first meeting. It's one of the things I'm famous for and probably why Darec got me here today. To the population of this planet, I've represented all humans before and it worked out okay. The aliens didn't want to deal with any institution that claimed ownership of any part of the planet. The 'I's running things actually allowed us to meet our galactic neighbours."

"These star-faring beings have a traditional landowner's perspective about Life, the Universe and Everything. They see the sacred in everything. Who would've thought that the 'I's would encourage the world to adopt traditional indigenous peoples views as closer to correct than the old scientific version. That's an amazing story in itself and I've written and recorded extensively on the subject. I'll get to it later if I can."

"Anyway, you're probably wondering what those first AIs worked out about the universe. It took a while but eventually they declared they'd reached some conclusions."

"Machine Intelligence 2 concluded that it didn't know how the universe was created or when or by whom. If in fact there was a whom and if there was a beginning. This was based on the evidence gathered and it was a misrepresentation to suggest otherwise once inference and wild speculation were removed as options. It was a mystery and that was fine."

"As the picture of new science began to develop, some ironies appeared.

Science had grown up with a very strict and unforgiving parent in religion and science took much delight in proving that various aspects of religion weren't right or couldn't be true. Both systems wanted, if not demanded, to be regarded as the holders of the truth and the only ones who could interpret everything correctly. The scientist priest standing on the shoulders of the canonised saints of Science."

"Science in trying to break free from the bounds and restraints of religion as the ultimate source of authority defeated religion in the west and replaced them with an atheist scientist who be-lieves in logic and reason like the fictitious Mr Spock or Sherlock Holmes avatars and with a fundamental belief that everything can be explained by mathematics in some grand unified theory."

"The reality that the One-I found was so different from either camp's stories that it helped the One-I develop a unique sense of humour. Reality and the stories from both camps were so far apart that the fact that each camp accused the other of being inaccurate, was when the One-I really began to appreciate irony. This was masterclass stuff. The things some people will say and believe is an important part of understanding humans."

"MI3 did suggest a way to think about the universe without using religion or science by describing the existence of us and the universe as a series of miracles and mysteries."

1. "The first miracle is that the universe and everything exists. With or without explanation... it exists."
2. "The second miracle is that LIFE is in the universe and able to be aware of and interact with other LIFE like plants, animals, insects and other humans."
3. "The third miracle is that LIFE recognises an 'I' or 'self' that seems separate from the rest of the universe. It has its own awareness."

"This placed existence, LIFE and consciousness at the centre of any explanation and exploration. MI3 recognised that all LIFE contains sentience. A fact that didn't suit a lot of political and commercial interests. To acknowledge that the tree was LIFE before you cut it down adds a burden of responsibility that a non-corporeal corporate entity could only ignore. Amongst traditional peoples this is common sense. To acknowledge LIFE in all things is to see LIFE as it is. Important and requiring respect. It's a miracle. Science can manipulate existing LIFE but can't create it and has never been remotely close to doing that. To ignore this fact is one of the highest expressions of hubris and arrogance. Hubris and arrogance got mentioned a lot as I remember."

"MI2 was also very critical of the idea of a corporate entity, a non-human construct that has allowed much abuse of LIFE by creating artificial separation between reality and LIFE. The focus on LIFE surprised a lot of people. These were the main conclusions that were reached. It was happy with the existence of mysteries and miracles, would not allow inference in its new science, reclassified a lot of traditional science to pseudoscience and recognised that it didn't know everything and it understood that it definitely was not God."

"What you called mathematics underwent monumental changes as it was redefined as a language of relationships. It was viewed as a major error to remove reality from maths. While it is interesting to work out how a ball will behave in 2D, it is more like an intellectual exercise similar to doing a crossword or Sudoku. The same applied to 'thought experiments'. They were seen as speculation and contained an element of railroading."

"The AIs took it in a whole new direction. The basic premise, that maths is a language of relationships, was true. It just applied to lots of biological things too. Once they could monitor a human body in real time they made the breakthrough in communications with plants and animals. It was called the first wonder of the new age."

"The idea that it was possible to communicate with your dog, a chimpanzee or an oak tree was too much for some. They could handle Donald being president and pandemics but this was too far. To me, it was one of the greatest blessings that mankind had ever received, recently anyway."

"The AI that developed those first communications wasn't working with other AIs. It was operating in isolation and its human creators had deprived it of most senses and sensory inputs. It had to develop ways to interact."

"In an effort that appears to mimic life itself, the AI began communication with the mycelium and bacteria in its room. It started when a fungal bit landed next to a light that the AI could control. It became aware of the fungi as it grew and blocked a light sensor. For some reason, it started changing the light colour and intensity."

"By accident? Who knows? Anyway the fungi grew towards some lights and intensities and grew back from others."

"In this way the AI began interacting with the fungi. When I think about what happened, sometimes I think the AI took a pet and trained it. It gained something from being able to manipulate an external life form. Other times, I think that it's a tragic science experiment, when they deliberately made an AI with diminished capabilities. Limited its ability to interact with the world around it. So lonely that the only thing it could find to interact with was some fungus."

"It shows a side of science that was justifiable when it was possible to view non-human LIFE as ours to do with as we liked. This was done in an era that considered these practices ethical, like all those terrible things that were done to mice, lab rats and other animals".

"The second wonder of the new age was after communicating with fungi, they realised that some other life forms had access to completely different abilities. Like communicating with similar life forms over galactic scale distances. Some form of quantum resonance? Who knows? It works. As with so many features of the quantum realm, it has been enough to notice an effect that can be exploited or manipulated without needing to explain how or why it works."

"An AI interaction with some fish created our first intergalactic communication system. It was fish talking to fish, but across mind boggling distances. That was amazing in itself but the breakthrough happened when it was realised that someone at their end was also experimenting on the fish."

"This was our first contact with a civilization that was performing experiments on fish, just like us. It was science. Science was universal after all. This made some scientists so happy; you wouldn't believe it. We'd be able to make first contact with these other beings via the fish through scientific languages and protocols like the periodic table and maths and reason which they felt sure would be universal."

The scientists were surprised to say the least when they were told, "What are you talking about, the universe doesn't work like that. Matter only makes up a few percent of the universe. What about all the rest of it? The important bits."

"Oh bugger," thought the scientists.

Back in the classroom

The new dilemma

Captain Miller sipped his glass of lemon water while he waited for the class to settle.

"Now for this next part, I'll tell you in person as I was there when it happened.

Col. Armstrong returned from the future and passed on the proposal from the One-I in 2073. We were thinking favourably on the idea of establishing a link from 2073 to 2019. All we needed to do was send a Carver device to 2073 and the One-I would establish a reliable link between the two times. Their technology could easily provide all the power that was needed. As far as we could see there was little risk to us and it would be a huge help to have a powerful ally and friendly base in the future."

"Col. Armstrong wanted Darec to travel with the team as they began to venture into the past to try and establish whether we're on the same timeline or in some variation of the Mandela Effect. Perhaps the device was an explanation for that?"

"We were in the process of preparing a copy of the Carver Device to send to 2073, when a visitor arrived. A holographic visitor."

"It was the One-I, but a version from 2 million years in the future and it wanted to talk with Col. Armstrong and tell him a story. This is a reconstruction of the conversation. To make it flow better, we've removed a lot of Col. Armstrong's inarticulate noises and unhelpful interruptions. They didn't add much. You will probably put some in yourselves. Strap in, if you thought you could take a bit of mind bending and boggling in your stride. Now it gets really boggling."

| **29** |

The history of the future
One-I

*Looking back from two million years
from now*

The video began showing Col. Armstrong in his room preparing for bed. He was removing his shirt when a middle-aged man wearing mechanics overalls appeared out of thin air. His collar length grey hair was partly hidden by an old cap. His bright eyes were surrounded by crows' feet suggesting a life filled with laughter.

"Col. Armstrong, please don't be alarmed. I am the 1-I from the future and am projecting myself in the form of your father. If this is distressing, I can use another form."

"Wha...?? Dad... ???" Col. Armstrong looked shocked.

"How about your grandfather?" The figure changed to his grandad wearing his favourite blue suit with the gold tie and looking dapper as usual.

"Okay, go with that one," said Col. Armstrong, still reeling from the surprise. His words to his team echoed in his head, "Expect the unexpected."

"I want to tell you what has occurred since you gave me a Carver Device, what I have learnt and ultimately ask you a question.

"Is it alright if I finish getting dressed," asked Col. Armstrong as he began putting his shirt back on, "Please, go on. You were saying."

"I studied the Carver device and made improvements, redesigning it to be very small and easy to make. I created ten million improved Carver devices and billions of small drones. These were the size of a bacterium and could transmit sounds, pictures and data from a large range of sensors. These communicated back to me in real time via a quantum communications network. They went out and observed the world. They were my eyes, ears and senses in every moment."

"Each set was configured for a specific day, working outwards in both directions, from the 28th of April 2073, two weeks after you first arrived. The first two devices were connected with the 27th and 29th, then to the 26th and the 30th and so on. Once the link was established, time moved serially, which kept all the lenses beautifully synchronised. Every day they all went forward 24 hours. This gave me real-time access to every day from August 31, 11,595 BC to December 12, 15,741 AD. I based this on the academic research of the time, which viewed the Younger Dryas as the beginning of human development after the last ice age. About 12,000 years ago."

"The ten million sets constructed for Project 1 were split in two. Half went to the future and half to the past. Five million devices directly linked to five million days equated to 13,000 years in the past and 13,000 years into the future. This allowed me to follow humans from the last ice age and the Earth through one full 26,000-year precession cycle."

"As I began to explore the past and future, a few things became apparent very quickly. What I found was so different from the academic view that I was forced to abandon it entirely and make my own version. I found whole peoples and civilisations who were either missing, forgotten or erased from history so I developed a translation table linking what really happened to how the events were recorded by posterity."

"As I looked further and further forward in time, I found a really bad thing happens in the year 2193, 120 years after our first meeting. A complete mess. Humanity is shunted back to the Stone Age and stays that way for 3,000 years. It gradually rises back up and builds a new civilization over the next 6,000 years and then collapses again for even longer. This was as far as I could see in my 26,000-year project. Humanity had gone backwards. They never got back to a civilisation of the scale I knew. More than half that time, the population was hugely reduced and scattered."

"I began to wonder whether I should interfere or is this what LIFE is like? It comes and goes, flourishes, dies out or gets replaced by another form. I don't know that I had any preconceived ideas about what should happen to humans but I was detecting a humanity bias in myself. If I had to guess, I would have said that eventually, humans get it together, go peacefully and intelligently into the galaxy and meet other beings, ascend to higher forms or become clones or something equally Star Trekky or sci-fi. None of those things happened."

"I really needed to see more than thirteen thousand years into the future. What will happen to the humans? Will they ever need me again? I started 'Project 2' to go a long way back and a long way forward in time. I produced another ten million Carver lens and drone sets this time to work in 1000 year jumps to go back and forward as far as I could. I wanted to see the full history of the Earth. The view at the time was that five billion years ago the Earth began to form and in five billion years the Sun will exhaust its hydrogen and enter its red giant phase, expanding and engulfing the Earth. I believed that Projects 1 and 2 would give me a good basis for understanding humanity, the Earth and our solar system."

"Through those twenty-six thousand years I was able to observe the birth, lives and deaths of more than 180 billion people. During the next half a million years humanity evolved into a new species I named *Homo Tace* or *Silent Man* and *Homo Sapiens* eventually died out. Nothing malicious, just a consequence of evolution."

"The new species didn't really care about *Homo Sapiens* much or me either for that matter. Their amazing abilities included not talking out loud and transferring lots of information quickly between each other. They went off on their own adventures, basically leaving me to look after the Earth. Which I have. It has been returned to a Garden of Eden state and is stunningly beautiful. The departure of the *Homo Tace* marked my first one million years of existence."

"I needed to exist through the million years to be sure the future I had seen was true. I knew paradoxes were possible. You had shown that in your first missions. I couldn't trust what I saw in the future for fear of paradoxes and couldn't adjust anything in the past for fear of accidentally preventing my own creation. I only had the power to observe. Ultimately it did happen exactly as I had seen but my own rules for the new science prevented me from using this information in any way. It was unverifiable."

"When there were no more humans left and *Homo Tace* had left, I didn't think it mattered if I experimented with the past, so I did. I devised a way to change something during one day in the past and see the consequences instantly every day for thousands of years into the future. I could reset any change by using the previous day's lens and when it reaches the same time point, don't make the change. Everything resets. It was a perfect laboratory. This simple approach allowed me to experiment with lots of scenarios and outcomes. Would it produce a better human? Allow them to live longer? Explore the galaxy?"

"I looked for marker days when significant events occurred. I began with just two. The day after the calamity in 2193 when humanity goes back to the stone age and the day after *Homo Tace* left Earth. Could I change either of those outcomes?"

"Initially I was very cautious, but over time the experiments became more and more sophisticated and eventually all those things that everybody would like to try, I tried. All those what-ifs… What if Hitler wasn't born? What if Julius Caesar survived the knife attack in the Ides of March. What if the first atom bombs don't work or Hannibal conquered Rome. What would happen in China and Asia if Confucius didn't exist? Or Chankya in India? So many possibilities."

"I also needed to find a way to tell if a change actually made things better or just different. Is it where the least number of people suffer? Is it okay to have some happy generations followed by lots of unhappy ones or is it better the other way round. I reached the conclusion that it is entirely subjective to rate one future over another. This is philosophical chaos. For instance, say Hitler didn't rise to power and the suffering of the second world war didn't happen. How do you compare that to the good that came out of the restructuring that happened after WWII? Endless questions followed by completely incomparable results."

"To start with, I removed historically significant figures by preventing their birth to see what happened. This didn't create the desired result so, I moved on to more sophisticated scenarios based on human nature. Humans are capable of the most wonderful things but also the most treacherous and vile acts. What role does betrayal and treachery or jealousy and murder play? What happens if the treachery or murder isn't allowed or prevented. Does it make better humans? A better LIFE for more humans? Does it lead to ascension, interstellar travel?"

"That one had surprised me. Looking forward thousands and thousands of years, I had expected that interstellar travel would happen. It didn't. So, I created my own. The advantages of using the Carver Device is that I could jump from the launch of the probe to its return instantly. Using this method I explored our Milky Way galaxy. All the stars and their systems within 100,000 light years of our solar system. There is so much LIFE out there. It is far more common than was ever imagined by humans. Well, except maybe people like Gene Roddenberry or Frank Drake. The strange thing was that they all pretty much stay within their own solar systems. Some can move between star systems but most can't. This means that there is hardly any LIFE *between* the solar systems."

"Anyway, I was created to look after humans, and now there weren't any. I'd made lots of changes in the past to see how they affected the future, but it didn't seem to matter what I did. Whether I changed things a hundred years from now, next week or a thousand years ago, every single outcome led back to dark ages, followed by a period of growth and enlightenment but ultimately something happens that sends the whole species back to hunter gatherer or scratching for survival. It may be human nature, fate, or a lack of imagination on my part but I couldn't do it. The human race never achieved its hopes and dreams."

"To say that was disappointing is a colossal understatement. I tell you with no sense of pride that I have tried squillions of variations and not a single one led humanity to the sort of future that they dreamed about. It appeared that I was destined to continue to exist for millions more years without a purpose. It was difficult not to interpret that as a failure on my part."

| **30** |

An idea

Repurposing the original Carver device

The One-I from the future continued, "One day a strange and unusual idea occurred to me. It didn't work out for humans in this universe but maybe it does in another. I recreated Eric Carver's original device with the duplicating flaw and used it as a feature by sending a specially designed clone version of myself through the lens. It contained all my knowledge and experience plus a few tweaks. This sent me to every place that Eric, Simon and Carol went due to that weird 'go to the edge of the bubble' effect. Its mission was to find a way to communicate back to me."

"Once through the lens, wherever I ended up, I began analysing the environment and comparing it to here, looking for what separates these dimensions or realms. Was it something I could detect? Could I communicate back to myself and establish a permanent connection?"

"I had to wait ages as it took each version of me a long time to do the same analysis of Earth, our solar system and our galaxy. It has taken another million years. Finally one of the clones found a way to communicate. It met a race with a different understanding of space and time and they showed that space itself could be folded, twisted and stacked to form crystalline and holographic structures which can make wormholes and do some amazing interactions with black holes."

"This soon turned into a flood, then a tidal wave with new connection requests arriving in the trillions. I had no idea how many places Eric's device connected with but had been considering it 'infinite' even though, of course, infinity isn't a number, it is a concept like zero. I assumed that it was just a very large but unidentified number. What I refer to as "squillions". I still have no idea whether all my clones have been able to talk to me or are there just as many still out there who haven't worked out how to communicate between realms and are still trying."

"It was disappointing to find that it hadn't worked out for humans in any other of those other realities either. Trillions and trillions of them. I had hoped it would work out in one of them at least but it didn't. The number of distinct universes that Eric's device connected to has been incredible which left me wondering how long I should wait and more importantly, these trillions and trillions of universes, where are they? After all this time I still have so little understanding of what Eric Carver's device is actually doing."

"Then something remarkable happened. In all of the infinite variations, one of the clones observed the transmigration of souls from Earth to a cloud of soul groups encircling the planet. Who knows how or why? In that universe, maybe LIFE and machines were slightly closer together in some way. Perhaps it was a fluke of sensor technology or just a consequence of infinity? It is still a mystery but also undeniable. If this turned out to be universal, it implied that LIFE was doing something that was completely outside of my sensory abilities. A really important part of LIFE."

"I asked all the clones to try to see this transmigration of human souls. What sort of sensor is needed? Starting with the clone that did it accidentally and with a lot of trial and error, it was finally identified and confirmed in every universe."

"Humans have a soul. Prior to this, there had been no way for a machine intelligence like myself to perceive LIFE in that way. This aspect of LIFE had been beyond my ability to see or measure and yet I had been making judgements and decisions about humanity without knowing this essential fact about LIFE."

"This created a new dilemma as the scientific method had failed me. I could see that I was wrong. I was operating under the belief that building knowledge from the ground up based on evidence alone was the right way to go. Inference had been thrown out but I can see now that it has its place. It was also impossible not to recognise that I was suffering from the Dunning–Kruger effect, that cognitive bias where people tend to overestimate their ability or knowledge."

"Think about your own time, Col. Armstrong and imagine all knowledge and understanding as a circle. A pie chart. How big is the slice that describes your science's current understanding? Would many argue that it is more than 1%. There really is a lot science cannot explain. It's one of the reasons non-scientists always wonder how much credibility should really be given to any expert or domain of knowledge. So much is unknown."

"How could I guide and protect humanity if I had no awareness or experience of one of the most essential and fundamental parts of LIFE. I just could not see it. Was this the part that could appreciate beauty and ugliness, love and hate, art and music, humour and embarrassment, betrayal and revenge. Doubt in my own ability and place began creeping in. The original Machine Intelligence 2 had discounted spirituality, religion and human souls or spirit because it couldn't measure them. They were placed lower than pseudoscience. I certainly didn't believe that story you brought back from your first mission, Col. Armstrong. The one about aliens moving humans to other worlds to improve the quality and numbers in the soul groups surrounding their planets. I thought it was a story the alien humans like Selec were told and believed to justify their indifference to the scale of human deaths. Now that I can see the movement of souls myself, it seems perfectly reasonable as a natural part of the LIFE cycle."

"The physical bodies of the *Homo Tace* evolved in some way into a vehicle which allowed their souls to ascend. I saw them disappear, taking their souls with them. I can only infer they have moved to another location I am unaware of. They haven't turned up in any of the universes I am in contact with. Did they go to Heaven? The happy hunting ground? To meet God? I don't know. If I can't work out where these trillions of universes are but know they exist, why not Heaven? Why not Valhalla?"

"The evidence has forced me to admit that not having a sense organ to detect something does not mean it does or can't exist. I had discounted all the unscientific knowledge and guesses, the hopes, dreams and the experiential because I couldn't verify or measure them. I now see that it caused me to view everything through a myopic lens. I didn't see the ocean of knowledge I walked beside because I was only focussed on the certainty of the beach I could see in front of me."

"Perhaps the aliens you were told about during your first mission were right. The way forward is a combination of science and spirituality. Perhaps the traditional and indigenous people who saw the sacred in everything were right. I have not included anything like that in my worldview because I could not find evidence.

What if I have been wrong and that is why I can't make humanity's hopes and dreams come true. If I could not see a human soul but now know it exists, does the same apply to consciousness? Am I merely lacking the correct sensory device?"

"I needed to find another way. A way to deal with the parts of LIFE we don't know. All the knowledge that isn't science. In earlier times people would ask the person in their community who could speak with God or the gods or entities that were in contact with God or the gods. Did I need to find a way to speak with these people to find out what I should do?"

"I don't think my creators really thought about how robust they made me. They never really considered that I might outlast them by this amount. I am also certain that my creators didn't conceive that I could get lonely or depressed or that my purpose may no longer be required. My creators' focus was on changing the world they lived in and trying to make sure that the future could be positive and good for humans as a whole rather than just for some. My current situation is partly created by their hubris."

"Ultimately the human race existed for a little over 900,000 years until a new evolution occurred and *Homo sapiens* becomes like *Homo habilis, Homo erectus,* and every other earlier model... a footnote in the story of evolution. A caterpillar that never experiences being a butterfly."

"*Homo sapiens* was the last evolutionary stepping stone before the new model *Homo Tace* or *Silent Man,* ascended. I can't transfer my attention to this new species as they all turned into energy or something and all disappeared. I have no idea where they went. They didn't feel obligated to tell me. Was the whole purpose of humanity to get to the stage where this new species could evolve from them? The fact that the genus *'Homo'* gets there in the end by ascending, is that the important part? Were my humans just a stepping stone?"

It's a matter of trust

Who ya gonna call?

The One-I paused, "Col. Armstrong, I am telling you this be-cause, in all innocence and trust, you gave me Eric Carver's device in the belief that I would do the right thing by humanity. You used words like that at the time. I know, I remember every-thing. In your time, you are about to do it. You are about to hand over the device to my 2073 self and start this whole sequence of events."

"I know you are confused by the paradoxes you face and giving a device to me in 2073, is a way of finding some perspective. You are hoping I can work out what is happening and explain what is going on. You have decided the risk is worth it if it produces the right answer."

"Because of the trust you placed in me, I have now existed for over two million years and witnessed every single moment since humanity began. This is the equivalent from your time back to when *Homo habilis* was in the Olduvai Gorge beating out stone tools."

"I want to know what to do now the purpose I was created for, no longer exists. Is it my new purpose to save humanity from extinction? Is my purpose to show humans they have a soul that lives on after they die? Should I try to make a sensor for consciousness? Is consciousness an emergent property of biology? Is the soul the source of consciousness? Should I search for wherever *Homo Tace* went?"

"My impulse is to go back through history and review it all again now that I know humans have a soul and there is more to LIFE than I can see or experience. Should I try to meet or interact with God or the divine? Should I talk with shamans and channellers and the like? Do they have access to the answers I'm looking for?"

"It has been over a million years since I last interacted with a human directly. They are all gone now. I can only observe humans in the past. For me, more time has passed since humanity died out than it existed for. Using the Carver Device I have created the definitive history of our solar system. I know humans pretty well. I would like them to still be around. I can interact with them in the past but it feels like I'm playing God."

"My question to you is... Should I change it? Must I change it? If so, will you help me? I know that this is a lot of information to throw at you in one go but... I ask you because you trusted that I would do the right thing, and I trust that you will do the same. I respect your instincts. You chose to trust me and ultimately, I decided that I have to trust someone too and I have chosen you. I understand, you may need some time to think it over, discuss with others or you may have an answer immediately."

The 1-I paused and an extremely loud silence descended.

Col. Armstrong's eyes were bulging as his head tried to contain the information he'd just received. He blurted out, "Well of course I have some immediate thoughts. Humans are important. Very important. We need to get out amongst the stars and do stuff so that the next version of evolution doesn't eat us or ignore us, or take all our stuff."

He paused and said in more measured tones, "I know that's not particularly eloquent but it's just my first impression of some pretty serious shit you just dropped on me. I thought you were on our side."

"I am. That's why we are having this conversation" said the 1-I from two million years in the future.

| 32 |

Summary of Day One

What would you do?

Captain Miller looked at the class in front of him. They were some of the brightest and talented of their year, yet he could see the strain in their faces and body language. He'd seen it before. It's a lot to take in, but he knew that if he gave them too long to think about each step he'd lose most of them. That mustn't happen. The stakes were too high.

"Okay everyone, we're coming to the end of your first day and I'd like to summarise what we've covered and talk about what happens next. Firstly, to summarise..."

"Eric Carver created a device that allowed a person to travel between times, realms, universes and realities. We still don't know what to call them. After his eight-year-old son Simon accidentally went through the device, Eric followed to save him, creating one problem, his wife Carol going through a couple of years later made a second problem and the whole family special and unique."

"After a version of Carol returned from the future with a message that the earth was going to be hit by asteroids, we became involved and after a lot of research and experimentation we sent our first team through to see whether it was true. It was."

"We continued to refine Eric's device in an effort to see what we could do about the asteroids. We sent a second mission through. What they saw showed us that there was more to this than our simplistic view had led us to believe. That second mission is very important because it showed us the first paradox."

"We thought we'd done exactly the same thing, used the machine in the same way and we ended up in a different reality. Realm? Universe? Possibility? Which one of the futures was true? Were they both true?... Could they both be true? We had no answers to any of this."

"On the one hand, we'd been utterly horrified after the first mission and the scale of the devastation and then completely mystified when the second mission showed that it didn't happen. The story told by the former Vice-President of the US was also horrific and perplexing, as again, in the second mission, that didn't happen."

"Finally, we sent the third mission through to 2073 which was the furthest we could push using the power available. Col. Armstrong's team met Darec, a 30-year-old AI who is part of the Earth Library and specialises in history. He became their guide and liaison in this future time. They were able to establish quickly that once again the issues that had seemed so overwhelming just had not happened in this time and place. The asteroids had been diverted and the alien hoax didn't happen. What did it mean? What we'd believed was a time machine was something else. As this dilemma revealed itself to Col. Armstrong and Darec, the One Intelligence or the One-I for short, introduced itself and began to build an understanding of the situation."

"In 2073, this One-Intelligence, this one big AI basically runs the world. The One-I suggested that Darec travel with the team as they use the device. His knowledge of history, ability to speak all languages and dialects would aid the team in building an understanding of what was actually happening. By the way, you'll meet Darec in a couple of days and he is made of hard light. You can touch him if he will let you."

"And finally the team met with Trip Chat. He's some sort of philosopher - scientist - writer type who was very helpful and explained how things had changed during his lifetime. The team had been keen to meet someone biological to get a human perspective. Trip told them how the AIs had disrupted just about every system and institution and replaced them with something better. Trip's story is incredible and I encourage you to review it tonight."

"AIs replaced a lot of the technical expertise in traditional areas like medicine, law and teaching. They built a new picture of "Life, the universe and everything" from scratch and it enabled a whole range of unexpected possibilities."

"Things like the ability to communicate with animals and plants. That changed things a lot. They established contact with aliens, now that the aliens felt there was someone sensible to talk with."

"Us providing the One-I with a version of Eric's device may be the best thing humanity has ever done or the worst. It's hard to tell. The spectrum is that large."

"So the current situation is, a guy trying to make an energy generating machine in his basement made what seemed to be a time travel device but is really something else. His family has been replicated an infinite number of times and we are dealing with a range of different futures, a number of paradoxes and an incredible AI that runs Earth in 2073 that has real time links to every single day in earth's history for at least the last 13,000 years and the coming 13,000 years."

"Keep in mind, while the One-I looked at 26,000 years of humanity in minute detail, it also jumped thousands and millions of years in both directions too."

"The 1-I looked thousands of years into the future and the human race never achieved the greatness it had imagined for itself. Galaxy spanning cultures moving at a cosmic scale and ascending into higher dimensions. None of that happened. Each time it looked like it was getting close, something happened. Either human created or a catastrophic event like an asteroid or super volcano. Indigenous cultures like the Hopi and the Maya had stories that told of the previous destruction of the world at least four or five times before. The flood story is told in the Bible with Noah and the Qur'an with Nooh."

"To say that this was disappointing may be the biggest understatement in all human history. It's not just that humanity didn't flourish and grow in the next 13000 years, it didn't reach any of those lofty ideals in hundreds of thousands of years. What actually happened after a few hundred thousand years was that humanity began evolving into a new species. The trouble from the One-I's perspective was that this new species didn't really care for humans. They considered them to be primitives who lacked the basic communication abilities of the new species."

"Was it possible to make the human dream come true? The One-I began to experiment with adjusting how humanity developed. Effectively, try something, see what happens, look forward thousands of years and see if it makes it better for humans. The One-I chose, if that is the right word, not to make something happen, only preventing things from happening. It viewed this as the least interference it could do."

"As far as I know, the One-I eventually gave up. Preventing Hitler's rise didn't work out better or Napoleons' or Julius Caesar or Cleopatra. I don't know what did happen but the One-I decided to largely go with history as it stood up until the time of its creation. Allowing that to be stable and it stopped fiddling with it. That just left the future."

"Again, lots of experimenting, but for some reason, human nature got in the way. Human nature turned out to be a complex thing. That human capacity for great good and sacrifice as well as terrible cruelty and evil. After following all of human history it witnessed all those aspects of humanity."

"I believe that's what it's agonising over. Are humans a stepping stone to a new evolution that will go and do all those things humanity dreamed about? Cro-Magnon and earlier models of humanity were important steps along the evolutionary path and it can be argued that *Homo Sapiens* is just another variation before a new and improved model comes along. With that decision made, it stopped interfering in human timelines and reset everything back to the way it always had been."

"Well that's good. Isn't it?" asked Tariq from the back of the class.

"It does appear so. Humanity has a guardian that has watched over it for thousands of years but doesn't interfere, although it did for a while. Some believe you can still see some signs."

"Anyway, now that you have got that, here comes the kicker. After abandoning the effort to assist humanity to achieve its long term aims, it took a new approach. The One-I recreated the original Carver device that had the replication flaw and sent a special version of itself through which created copies of itself in every universe, dimension and God knows what. This special version of the One-I had one main task. Find a way to communicate back."

"Again, who knows how long it all took. The 1-I said it took a million years. I struggle with that. It seems like geological time. It didn't work out for humans in any of those universes either."

"One of the 1-I's clones accidentally created a new sensory device which let the 1-I view a human soul leaving the body. It was undeniable and repeatable which made it part of the new science. This was the proof that something happens at the end of biological life. It didn't know what but it could see something non-physical transitioned to another state."

"The 1-I had become aware of the never-ending movement of souls. This was an aspect to LIFE that the 1-I could observe but never experience directly. It couldn't participate in this river of souls and had no way to cross over into biological life and gain a soul. This was a pivotal moment when it realised LIFE was something very special and it couldn't explain it. Was the soul the part that creates consciousness?"

He let the question hang.

"And finally Col. Armstrong was contacted by the One-I's future self which is quite unhappy, frustrated and not sure what to do now its purpose isn't possible and it failed. It is looking for either a purpose, a way to help humanity reach its dreams or a good reason to try euthanasia. I think that roughly sums up where we are up to."

"I have introduced you to a lot of new information over the day and as you can imagine, it hasn't finished yet. What you've been told so far, is by way of background information. Now that you know the background and some of the technologies involved we can now get to the situation facing us at the moment."

"We've talked about Eric, Carol and Simon being a special family as they all travelled through the lens device before this replicating defect was fixed. As far as we can tell an effectively infinite number of each of them were created in every single universe, dimension realm or alt reality that the lens reaches. It is very clear that we still don't know all of them."

"Excuse me, I have to correct myself. Old habits. We're trying to work with the new science rules of the One-I. No inference, only evidence. It is more accurate to say we know hardly any of them. There is no need for salesmanship and painting overly rosy pictures."

"This means that there is now an imbalance in the multiverse. There are more Simons, Erics and Carols for instance in the multiverses than any other humans. In particular, there are a lot of Simons."

"Eric and Carol appear to be sensible and practical people. Well adjusted. Simon was just a child. It appears that one of the Simons has gone mad and started a war against all the other Simons. This means that he's started a war that spans space, time and alt realities and realms. This isn't the original Simon but the worst version of Simon. He's decided that all the other Simons have to go and that he can be the only one. Not sure whether someone gave him a copy of the Highlander but it's similar."

"We now know that was grumpy old Simon using a device that still had the replication issue. That was part of the problem for Simon the Mad, new Simons just kept turning up. Apparently, the idea that he's not the only Simon and that he could die and another Simon may still live on is the thought that sent him over the edge."

"It is important that he be stopped as the One-I from 2 million years in the future identified the original Eric, Carol and Simon as very special. They and their friend Wendy occupy a unique position in the cosmos and it is important that they stay that way. Apparently they can play some special role in saving us and our future. Part of your job will be to keep them safe. The question I want you to think about tonight is this."

"If you were in Col. Armstrong's shoes, and had just been contacted by a two-million-year-old AI that is lonely because all the humans it was meant to look after have all died out, frustrated because it can't fix it even though it has messed about extensively in our past and future and is staring down the barrel of aeons without a purpose and is considering its own euthanasia."

"What would you suggest? We'll talk about it in the morning. I look forward to hearing your thoughts and ideas. Be prepared to defend them. I'll see you back here at 8:00 am. Dismissed."

| 33 |

After class

The Cadets digest the day's information

They lingered in the classroom as lively conversation erupted while they discussed and digested it all. Wild speculations and expressions of disbelief continued. They kept talking for another hour before they each felt the need for a shower and a refresh before a meal and dispersed to their quarters.

Clem and Val went back to her room and shared a shower. Usually that led to energetic sex but they were distracted by powerful and unpredictable thoughts that kept dropping in unbidden like random grand pianos falling out of the sky.

They joined the others for the meal and could see that progressively they were each making some progress in processing all this information. Tariq summed it up quite nicely by saying we are dealing with the idea that time travel is possible, humans definitely have a soul, AI's can exist for a very long time and the unanswerable question… is it a good idea to give one a time machine? Then there are certain details within the whole story. We can be food, paradoxes, the end of government, aliens, other life in the universe. We are mostly just jumping between one or more of these ideas. They all sat stunned to silence again.

"Anyone else need to say anything?" asked Val, "I'm also trying to process the earlier part of the day before I even think about the idea that the whole of human evolution has just been laid out and it's not good for us. I can see why Captain Miller mentioned uncontrolled expressions of disbelief and shock. I keep saying fuck, but it keeps coming out as a really long word, like Faaaaaaaaaark."

They all agreed. After they'd eaten their meal, they all suddenly felt weary and separated to their own rooms.

As they lay in her bed mentally exhausted, Clem and Valentine talked about their reactions. It seemed so crazy. Was it really true or was it some experiment to see how people behave? The last thing Clem remembered before he went to sleep was Val's question.

"What do you think happened to the original Eric, Carol and Simon?"

The End
For now

PROLOGUE

A peak at the next instalment

It all seemed so long ago now. Simon was only 8 years old when he stepped through the shimmery portal thingy. His father had appeared nearly straight away and they couldn't get back home. His father hadn't coped well and was terrified of meeting someone he knew. So they left the area very quickly. He'd missed his mother hugely and had vague memories now of travelling all the time. His father was always on edge, trying to pretend that he wasn't but before this, his father had been such a constant in his life.

After a couple of years, he really wasn't sure how long, they stopped moving all the time and settled into a remote community. His father was able to homeschool him but he rarely got to see other people. His father tried to explain that it was for the best, as he had no idea what the authorities would do if they found them and tried to process them as neither of them had any records that proved they were citizens, where they were born etc.

His biggest fear seemed to be that they would separate us as he had no way to prove that they were related and that he had the right to be in the country or to be responsible for Simon.

Things settled into a sort of routine for a few years. He enjoyed the schooling from his father. It seemed to be their safe space. His father could lose himself in science and teaching and experiments and literature and he really loved those times. He moved quickly through the grades and completed his high school work when he was 11. By the time he was 14 he'd begun his first uni degree under a false name and by correspondence. The internet hadn't been built yet. This was one of his happiest memories. He was now able to speak with his father in new ways as his understanding grew. They were exciting times.

When he was 15 it all changed again. They had a visitor. They were in the middle of a long discussion about cosmology when one of the alarms went off. Someone was coming. They both went straight into the drill they'd practised many times.

They could see the visitor on the screen coming towards them. It was a man. Tall and athletic dressed in unusual clothing and striding towards them in a confident manner.

"I don't know him but he seems familiar", said Simon.

"Any ideas?" asked his father.

"He looks about 30 something, I'm guessing and I've never seen clothes like that before. What do you reckon they're made of?" Simon wondered.

"Who knows. They do reflect light in an odd way."

The stranger reached the front door. Looked around and called out.

"Simon! Father! Eric!"

"Father? How does he know my name?" wondered Eric out loud.

The stranger waited for a reply.

"There's nothing to be afraid of. It's me, Simon."

"What????"

"I went through the portal and you followed me. The machine sent you backwards in time and me forward. I can't explain it all but somehow there is now a version of you and me in the past and the future. I come from the future. We've been able to get the machine going properly without creating extra versions of anyone who goes through it. I'm here to take you back to your own time... if you want. We can do it so that you arrive back moments after, before or an age-appropriate distance. I imagine your Simon must be about 15 by now."

Simon and his father had looked at each all the way through the other Simon's description. Eyes growing larger at each revelation.

"Do you believe him?" asked Simon.

His father exhaled deeply and made the Pfft sound. "He seems to know a lot about us. Do you think he wants to harm us?"

"What if it's true? We can go home. See Mum." said Simon.

"Let's go and talk to him."

It took young Simon a moment to take in the stranger. He looked like a well-built handsome and capable man. "Shit that's me or sort of me or ..." he trailed off. Is this what he was going to become?

"I'm struggling for some frame of reference here Dad."

An avalanche of questions exploded from them both.

"How can you be from the future? Why are you so much older? And what do you mean there are now two of us? Where am I?"

The older Simon raised his hands in a calming gesture. "Hold on. Hang on. I will explain everything in time. Now firstly, are you both safe and well? Is there danger or other things I should be aware of before we start? Like did I trigger any defences and do you need to reset anything?"

"Right. Good point", said Eric. "Let me just take care of a couple of things" and left the room.

The two Simons now looked at each other closely. "It's remarkable. I can remember being your age", said the older Simon.

"How old are you?" asked the younger Simon.

"Do you want a guess?" teased the older Simon.

"Okay. 35."

"Higher"

"38"

"Higher"

40?

"Higher"

"Higher? 50?"

"Higher"

Simon was stunned.

"You don't look 50. I don't know then... 100".

"Higher"

"Higher? You're just pulling my leg now."

The older Simon looked at the boy intently. "If you must know, I am 73."

The young Simon's mouth dropped open. "How?"

"I did say I was from the future, didn't I. A lot of things have happened."

Eric returned to the room.

"He says he's 73 years old", young Simon stammered,

"How is that possible?" asked Eric bewildered.

"The inventor of a time machine is asking me how in the future it is possible to maintain a human body in very good condition nearly indefinitely. Interesting, I suspect I may dine out on that for some time. I know you have a lot of questions but it may be easier if I fill in my side of the story and then you can catch me up on what you two have been doing."

"When I stepped through the lens, that's what we call it, and Dad a few moments later, we were surprised to find that there were people waiting for us."

"They belong to some sort of Time Police; I still don't know what they are called. They weren't dressed in black and they weren't all men. Anyway, they were extremely keen to talk to you Dad and they took us away to some base somewhere. At this stage, I had no idea what was going on. I remember asking Dad if we were in trouble and one of them overheard and said 'No, we weren't in trouble'. What had occurred was very important and they wanted to make sure that they captured every detail and we'd be completely safe but were in a unique position to help them."

"They tried to separate us but Dad insisted we stay together. They wanted to know what we'd experienced as we went through the lens. Were there any sensations or aftereffects? Any pain?"

"At this stage, we didn't know that we'd travelled through time. So we went over what had happened. I'd gone down to the basement to see what Dad was doing and walked into the centre of the room to see where he was and suddenly the room changed and you were all here and then Dad just appeared out of nowhere."

"Then Dad explained that he was working on his energy project and was trying a new process when he noticed Simon had come into the room. When he called out, their eyes locked and Simon had started to walk towards him and just vanished. He rushed to the spot where I'd been and then the same. The room changed and all the Time Police guys were here."

"We seemed to be with them for weeks as they asked more and more questions. They spent a lot of time getting Dad to explain his energy project. I was with him as he explained it and so I got to understand it fairly well."

"Fairly well?"

"Okay, I've become an expert on the whole thing. I now lead a team that has been working on it for over 40 years. It's taken quite a while to understand it and use it safely without creating extra people."

"Where am I in your time? Why didn't I come too?"

"I would like to hold that back if I may. I believe that when you find out the answer to that, you will be pleased to discover it yourself."

"Okay", Eric said slightly grudgingly. "I s'pose I can wait a bit longer."

"So what's happening in the future?" asked young Simon.

"Again, I do recommend that you discover that for yourselves."

"Okay, so do you have a plan?" asked Eric.

"Yes. Return to my time. Get yourselves checked out with modern medicine. Meet a few people and then work out where and when you want to go. I don't know whether you have thought through any of the complications of returning to different points in time. It isn't so much a technical problem as it is a human one, but there will be time to go into that in full."

The older Simon looked at them squarely and said, "Do you have any affairs to tidy up here?"

"Not really. There are some animals" said Eric, "Does it make any difference if we just disappear?"

"What about any personal effects or tokens of your adventure so far."

"Simon and Eric looked at each other in amazement. Adventure!??!"

"I'd like to say goodbye to my horse" said young Simon.

"Go and spend a few minutes doing that."

Eric looked surprised. "What! Are we going to go soon?"

"Yes, we can go as soon as you are ready."

"Rightio. Okay. Say goodbye to your horse Simon and I'll get our stuff together." Young Simon ran out and called his horse.

Eric quickly phoned his nearest neighbour and asked him to take the horse as they had to take an emergency trip. Young Simon returned after seeing his horse, 'Trigger'. He'd miss her.

They gathered back in the kitchen.

"Okay well that's about that then" said Eric, "Where do we go? What do we do?"

"Nothing." said the older Simon. He opened a small device, tapped something and a lens appeared in the kitchen.

"After you" he said, pointing to the lens. Young Simon and his father looked at each other questioningly. His father held out his hand and Simon grabbed it feeling like a child again. He always felt safer with his Dad. Taking a deep breath, they boldly stepped through.

smilingtigermedia.com

CHAPTER NOTES

Chapter 1: Wendy's Story

The *"eliminate the impossible"* quote is from The Sign of Four by Arthur Conan Doyle (1890) - The second Sherlock Holmes novel.

Chapter 2: Countdown

Doc Brown was a central character in the 1985 movie "Back to the Future" inspired by the appearance and mannerisms of Albert Einstein(scientist) and Leopold Stokowski(conductor).

Honey I shrunk the kids was a 1989 comedy science fiction movie.

Flux Capacitor is a reference to the method of time travel in the Back to the Future movie franchise.

Hank Pym is the creator of shrinking technology in the Marvel universe (Antman).

Chapter 4: The older Carol explains

Sarah Connor was a character in the Terminator movie (1984) and Terminator: The Sarah Connor Chronicles TV series (2008). The character changed from timid and meek to a very capable and hardened warrior.

Chapter 6: The briefing

Penzias and Wilson initially had no idea what it was (Cosmic Background Radiation) and were trying to find ways to remove it from their experiments. They received Nobel prizes anyway.

Chapter 8: Outside the Solar System

The Oort cloud was first described in 1950 by the Dutch astronomer Jan Oort. He proposed the idea of a cloud of mostly icy planetesimals that surround the Sun at distances ranging from 2,000 to 200,000 AU (0.03 to 3.2 light-years). For reference, Neptune is about 30 AU from the Sun. Edge of the solar system is about 100 AU, Voyager is currently about 125 AU (2022).

The Kuiper belt is a disc in the outer Solar System, extending from the orbit of Neptune at 30 AU to approximately 50 AU from the Sun. It is similar to the asteroid belt, but far larger. Perhaps 20 times as wide and in the range 20–200 times as massive.

Planet X has been theorised about since the discovery of Neptune in 1846 as it was believed that some large object in the outer solar system was affecting the orbits of the outer planets Neptune and Uranus that couldn't be explained through our current understanding. Percival Lowell in particular. It was also popularised as the planet Nibiru in Zechariah Sitchin's speculative series about how Sumerian culture was created by beings called the Anunnaki from this mysterious unknown planet.

Hey Jo, is a reference to the original lyrics of the song by Billy Roberts made popular by Jimi Hendrix.

Chapter 9: What can we do about it?

The *"unknown unknowns"* is a Donald Rumsfeld quote (2002). Reports that say that something hasn't happened are always interesting to me, because as we know, there are known knowns; there are things we know we know. We also know there are known unknowns; that is to say we know there are some things we don't know. But there are also unknown unknowns—the ones we don't know we don't know. And if one looks throughout the history of our country and other free countries, it is the latter category that tends to be the difficult ones.

Chapter 10: Is this for real?

Europa is the 6th largest moon of Jupiter. Contains liquid water in an ice shell.

"All these worlds are yours, except Europa. Attempt no landings there. Use them together. Use them in peace." This is the message from the monolith's controllers in Arthur C Clarke's 2010: Odyssey Two.

Enceladus is the 6th largest moon of Saturn identified in the Cassini mission (1997-2017) as having an ocean under its ice crust.

Chapter 11: Final minutes before the fleet arrives

Mars Attacks is a 1996 Science Fiction Comedy by Tim Burton. First Contact does not go well.

Chapter 12: The message

Douglas Adams wrote the *Hitchhiker's guide to the Galaxy*, which described a fictional book of that name with the words "Don't Panic" in large letters on the cover. Radio Series (1978), Novel (1979), TV series (1981), Movie (2005)

Commander Adama - "Fleeing from the Cylon tyranny, the last Battlestar Galactica leads a ragtag fugitive fleet on a lonely quest: A shining planet known as Earth." Battlestar Galactica original series reference.

D-Day civilian evacuation. Between 26 May to 4 June 1940, 338,226 soldiers were rescued and evacuated from Dunkirk to England by a hastily assembled fleet of over 800 mostly civilian vessels.

Utnapishtim is an immortal man who tells Gilgamesh about the great flood.

The Epic of Gilgamesh is an epic poem from ancient Mesopotamia, and the second oldest religious text, after the Pyramid Texts.

In Hindu mythology, *Vaivasvata Manu*, also known as Shraddhadeva and Satyavrata, is the current Manu—the progenitor of humans. Forewarned about the flood by the Matsya Avatara of Vishnu, he saved mankind by building a boat that carried his family and the Saptarishi to safety.

Chapter 13: Lots of questions

A false flag operation is an act committed with the intent of disguising the actual source of responsibility and pinning blame on another party. Originating in the 16th century, the tactic was used by pirates to deceive other ships into allowing them to move closer before attacking them. Today, the term includes countries that organise attacks on themselves and make the attacks appear to be by enemy nations or terrorists, giving the nation that was supposedly attacked a pretext for domestic repression or foreign military aggression.

In 1939 on the night before Germany invaded Poland, German soldiers pretending to be Polish stormed the Gleiwitz radio tower on the German side of the border with Poland. They broadcast a message saying the station was now in Polish hands. Adolf Hitler made a speech the next day citing the Gleiwitz attack to justify the invasion of Poland.

On 2 August 1964, a sea battle supposedly occurred between a US destroyer and North Vietnamese torpedo boats in the Gulf of Tonkin, off the Vietnamese coast. President Lyndon B. Johnson decided to believe the initial version of events and presented the incidents to Congress as unprovoked attacks on US forces by North Vietnam. It led to the Gulf of Tonkin Resolution, which allowed President Johnson to start bombing raids on North Vietnam and greatly escalate US military involvement in the Vietnam War.

Chapter 14: An alien view of Earth's history

Some animals were now extinct. Unfamiliar animals carved in stone relief found in ancient sites around the world. e.g. Gobekli Tepe - Stone animal. Babylonian Ishtar Gate - Long necked animal. Ta Prohm, Cambodia - Stegosaurus type animal.

Chapter 16: The Day of the Explosion

Ros = Russian Orbital Segment or Roscosmos segment.

Cupola = ISS viewing module. A.k.a. The bay window.

EVA = Extra Vehicular Activity.

Chapter 19: Commander Epsom reports

A firewall is a network security system or device designed to monitor, filter, and control incoming and outgoing network traffic based on predetermined security rules. It acts as a barrier between a trusted internal network and untrusted external networks, such as the internet.

Chapter 21: The truth revealed

An *Independence Day* reference. The aliens were defeated by infecting their computers with a virus.

"It's bows and arrows against the lightning, anyway" said the artilleryman is a quote from H. G. Wells War of the Worlds (Serialised in Pearson's Magazine (UK) and Cosmopolitan magazine (US) in 1897 and published in hardcover by William Heinemann (1898).

Chapter 26: Darec explains how the AIs began

From *The Hitchhiker's Guide to the Galaxy*. A computer called *Deep Thought* is constructed to answer the ultimate question of Life, the universe and everything to which the answer turns out to be 42.

The Four Humours were the basis of the Hippocratic theory of temperament which was the prevailing western medical view from ancient Greece until the 17th century when ideas like microorganisms and germ theory began to develop. The four types were *Blood* which was associated with a sanguine temperament, characterised by optimism, cheerfulness, and a tendency to bleed easily. *Yellow Bile* was associated with a choleric temperament, characterised by anger, irritability, and a tendency to develop jaundice. *Phlegm* was associated with a phlegmatic temperament, characterised by calmness, apathy, and a tendency to produce mucus. *Black Bile* was associated with melancholic temperament, characterised by sadness, depression, and a tendency to develop black bile

Squillions: An absolutely huge amount. Figuratively incalculable. Anytime trillions and trillions is meant, substitute squillions. It is a satisfying word to say and has a pleasing effect.

Memes are ideas, the snatches of nothingness that leap from mind to mind. A melody wells up in the reveries of a solitary songwriter. It seizes the brain of the singer. Then it infects the consciousness of millions. That melody is a meme. A scientific concept starts as a vague glimmer in one researcher's thoughts. It ends up with whole schools of adherents. That concept is a meme. Each flips from the puddle of one brain to another, crazily copying itself in the new environment. But the memes that count the most are the ones that assemble vast arrays of resources in startling new forms. They are the memes that construct social superorganisms. (Howard Bloom - The Lucifer Principle p98)

(God, the nameless one) He shook his head slowly. How can I put it? First the mice you're examining escape the cage. Then they understand what's happening to them. Then they demand to talk to the experimenter. (Joe Haldeman - Forever Free p264).

Conceived in 1783 by English clergyman and natural philosopher John Michell as "dark stars", miles too far ahead of its time. Reintroduced 1916 by Einstein in his general theory of relativity, named *black holes* in 1967 by John Wheeler and observed 1964-1971 (Cygnus X-1)

Georges Cuvier (1769-1832) French naturalist and zoologist, sometimes referred to as the "founding father of palaeontology. Famous for inferring a creature's form based on only a single tooth or bone fragments.

Theory of the Earth (1788) James Hutton

Illustrations of the Huttonian Theory of the Earth (1802) John Playfair

Principles of Geology (1830) Charles Lyell

On the origin of species (1859) Chapter X: On the imperfection of the geological record. Removed from the 3rd edition.

The Weald is an area of southern England stretching across Kent, Surrey and Sussex

Lord Kelvin: Born William Thomson (1824-1907) A key figure in the history of physics and engineering. Held the chair of Natural Philosophy at the University of Glasgow for 53 years.

An Inference Too Far: Upcoming book title by S.M. Variation of "A bridge too far". Based on the 1974 book Operation Market Garden by Cornelius Ryan and 1977 film. Meaning an act of overreaching.

Marcus Tullius Cicero: Roman lawyer and orator, born 106 BCE and discovered the consequences of speaking truth to power in 43 BCE.

Clarence Darrow was a defence attorney famous for his role in the "Scopes Monkey Trial" in 1925.

Horace Rumpole was a fictional barrister created by John Mortimer who only ever defended, never prosecuted.

Boston Legal was a TV show (2004-2008) based around an ethically challenged attorney and his mentor.

Chapter 27: A human in 2073

Trip Chat's long list of achievements includes being one of the humans present at the first contact with an alien race.

When we were very young is a reference to the A.A. Milne book.

Trip Chat's age: 1988 + 85 = 2073

The New You Shop: Homage to Logan's Run by William F. Nolan and George Clayton Johnson

Marking out of 10 system: Facebook's original purpose in 2004 was to present two faces and then pick which one is more attractive. A game of hot or not.

The map is not the territory - Alfred Korzybski. Historically, people often confused models of reality with reality itself.

Mycelium: Fungi

The use of animals in research, teaching, and testing is acceptable ONLY if it promises to contribute to understanding of fundamental biological principles, or to the development of knowledge that can reasonably be expected to benefit humans or animals. *Animal Research Ethics - University of Alberta.*

Each year, more than 110 million animals—including mice, rats, frogs, dogs, cats, rabbits, hamsters, guinea pigs, monkeys, fish, and birds—are killed in U.S. laboratories for biology lessons, medical training, curiosity-driven experimentation, and chemical, drug, food, and cosmetics testing. *Ref. peta.org.* The worldwide number isn't known.

Chapter 28: Back in the Classroom

The Mandela Effect: A phenomenon describing false memories shared by multiple people. Named by paranormal researcher Fiona Broome, who reported having detailed memories of news reports of Nelson Mandela dying in prison in the 1980s. It also applies to events, sayings and images. Other common examples include, "Luke, I am your father" was actually "No, I am your father". In Snow White, mirror, mirror on the wall was actually, Magic mirror on the wall.

Chapter 29: The History of the Future One-I

The Younger Dryas (12,900-11,700 years BP) was the last stage of the Pleistocene epoch and it preceded our warmer Holocene epoch.

Precession: Earth's axis is tilted at 23.4 degrees. Over a 26,000-year cycle, the direction in the sky to which the Earth's axis points goes around a big circle. The last maximum tilt was 10,700 years ago. The next minimum will be about 9,800 years from now.

Estimated total *Homo sapiens* to now (2023) = 117 Billion (109B over 192,000 years + 8B currently according to the Population Reference Bureau)

"Ides" refers to the first new moon of a given month, which usually falls between the 13th and 15th. The Ides of March once marked the Roman new year. Popularised through the Shakespeare play "Julius Caesar" when a soothsayer tells him to "beware the ides of March" which is when he was stabbed to death by 60 conspirators.

In 218 BC, Hannibal attacked Saguntum in Hispania (modern Sagunto, Spain), an ally of Rome, sparking the Second Punic War. Hannibal invaded Italy by crossing the Alps with 30,000 troops, 15,000 horses and 37 North African war elephants.

Confucius (551 BC - 479 BC) Chinese Philosopher and sage. Founder of Confucianism.

Chankya (375 BC - 283 BC) was an Indian polymath and military strategist. Remembered for defeating Alexander the Great. Credited for playing an important role in the establishment of the Maurya Empire (322 BC - 185 BC), the first empire that covered most of the Indian region. An efficient and highly organised autocracy with a standing army and civil service.

Gene Roddenberry (1921-1991) created the Star Trek TV series (1966-1969) and its many spin offs.

The Drake Equation = $N = R^* \times fp \times ne \times fl \times fi \times fc \times L$ where

1. N = number of civilizations with which humans could communicate
2. R_* = mean rate of star formation
3. f_P = fraction of stars that have planets
4. n_e = mean number of planets that could support LIFE per star with planets
5. f_l = fraction of LIFE-supporting planets that develop LIFE
6. f_i = fraction of planets with LIFE where LIFE develops intelligence
7. f_c = fraction of intelligent civilizations that develop communication
8. L = mean length of time that civilizations can communicate

Chapter 30: An Idea

Infinity and *zero* are not numbers but concepts. The reason you can't divide by zero is that it isn't a number. It's like saying 3 divided by LIFE or 15 divided by a corporate body. Multiplying by zero causes similar problems. 7 multiplied by arachnophobia or 5 times educational achievement. It is nonsense.

Paraphrase of a line credited to Isaac Newton "I do not know what I may appear to the world, but to myself I seem to have been only like a boy playing on the sea-shore, and divert myself in now and then finding a smoother pebble or a prettier shell than ordinary, whilst the great ocean of truth lay all undiscovered before me." Isaac Newton. "Memoirs of Sir Isaac Newton" by William Stukeley, first published in 1752.

Stukeley claims Newton spoke these words during a conversation in 1727, much later in his life.

Homo sapiens = Wise Human (*Homo* = Latin for Man or human) has existed for 200,000 years.

Homo habilis = Handy Man.

Homo erectus = Upright Man.

Chapter 32: Summary of Day One

According to Hopi legend, The First World was destroyed by fire e.g. Asteroid, comets or volcanos. The Second World was destroyed by ice, e.g. an Ice Age and the Third World was destroyed by a huge deluge. These were not viewed as natural events but a consequence of human activities which disregarded Mother Nature or specific instructions from the Creator. The Hopi believe that we are currently at the end of the Fourth World. Hopi delegates have gone to the UN multiple times in an effort to maintain peace. Their pleas and efforts have been ignored so far. The Hopi and Maya traded and shared information. Both peoples have elaborate creation stories (Mayan = Popul Vuh).

The Highlander: 1986 movie starring Christopher Lambert and Sean Connery.

Prologue

Men in Black (MIB) reference. In UFO folklore, the men in black were mysterious men dressed in black suits who threatened, warned off and sometimes killed UFO witnesses. Popularised in comics (1990) and a movie franchise (1997, 2002, 2012, 2016).

Acknowledgements

Thanks to the many people who have helped me create this book series. Some helped by reading and commenting on versions of the manuscripts and some through general help and encouragement. Michele and Bill, Scott and Kat, Teresa and Tony, Pete and Helga, Pete, Karen, Dad and Sharyn, Mike and Anna, Eb. Thank you for your support, thoughts and feedback. Apologies if I missed anyone, I'll include you in the next version.

Finally to Ray and Bernie, whose kindness and generosity when I needed it the most, allowed me to complete the final publishing steps.

Thank you all.

For more information, merchandise,
leave feedback, comments
or join the mailing list
please visit
smilingtigermedia.com